THE WOMEN

A Raising Women Expansion Pack

SHANNON WAITE

Shannon Waite
Detroit, Michigan

ABOUT THE AUTHOR

Award-winning writer and educator Shannon Waite writes stories about norms, characters who break norms, and society's wounds. They're always contemporary, often transgressive. Her debut novel, *Raising Women*, is an interactive novel in which readers make self-destructive decisions that explore the wild that is growing up girl.

Her short fiction has been published in *Pank*, *Hobart*, and elsewhere. She has two bachelor's degrees in English and Creative Writing from Oakland University and an MA in Teaching and Curriculum from Michigan State University. She lives in Michigan with her husband, cat, and hamster.

Visit her online at www.shannonwaiteauthor.com
@shannonwaiteauthor (Facebook and Instagram)
shannonwaiteauthor@gmail.com

BEFORE READING *THE WOMEN*

Content Warnings: *Note, this collection contains sensitive themes and subject matter that some readers may find disturbing. If you would like more information about sensitive content before reading, please check the detailed content guide on page 245.*

Both a prequel and sequel to Shannon Waite's interactive novel *Raising Women*, *The Women* is a collection of linked stories that allow readers to enter the self-loathing and self-destructive minds of eleven girls from the original novel. Watch as they become defiant women, unruly mothers, and unsavory wives.

While this collection does expand on the original novel's characters, it is a gritty, unsettling, and brave short story collection that can be read before, after, or isolated from the novel.

MORE ABOUT *RAISING WOMEN*

In *Raising Women*, you are on the precipice of womanhood and have become obsessed with an ex-convict, Roman. She introduces you to the dangerous and honest side of life that no one else has been able to. As she unapologetically places you in scandalous situations, you begin making self-destructive decisions. Depending on which decisions you choose, you may taste Roman's blood, get branded with a searing screwdriver, or date a married man— all while each choice challenges what it means to be a woman, real, or both.

In this interactive novel, readers have twenty-four possible pathways with four unique endings to explore the wild that is growing up girl.

TABLE OF CONTENTS

MISSING MARILYN

YOU WERE A POSTER CHILD. Your mother said so as you stood in line for your prize at the local strip mall arcade. You asked if poster children were sick, because you had heard that once, and she said not always. Sometimes they are sick, sometimes they are suffering, and sometimes they are the ideal. She said that you're a poster child for desire. You were an eight-year-old little girl, after all.

A boy ran past, shouting that he was a winner, as a flood of colors like skin and guts— reds, oranges, and browns—flashed and crashed around him, swallowing him whole. Sounds like gunshots erupted, race car engines roared, and *Cruisin' USA* and *Time Crysis* crowded the space. Ding ding ding.

Your mother shifted her shoulders, straightened up, and pulled the neckline of her shirt down, exposing skin as she stared at the man handling the prizes.

You tapped her arm. Just two people away from the counter. She said, "What?" exasperated as mothers are.

The walls were covered in movie posters: *Casablanca's* couple-stare, *The Three Stooges'* grins, *Top Gun's* jets. You pointed behind the man at the counter where a large, black and white image of a woman wearing tight, platinum-blonde curls, bent forward in a dress that spread like blooming flower petals, was displayed. Her eyes were closed and she was alone. Something about her looked embarrassed, but no one wants to see that, so she smiled. Fragile.

You said to your mother, "Look at her." She rolled her eyes. You asked, "Who is she?"

Your mother didn't look at you. She continued tracing the neckline of her shirt, pulling it lower, because she was the type to finish what she started before giving in.

A girl at the front of the line walked away with a small, pink teddy bear after turning in hundreds of tickets.

One more person to go.

After finally removing her hand from her chest, your mother said, "Marilyn Monroe."

So you asked again, "Who is she?"

She licked her fingers, making them wet with spit, and traced them along her collarbones. You liked how shiny they looked.

"I will only tell you who she is if you promise to never bring her up again."

You promised.

From the side of her mouth, your mother said, "She was a waif. Tossed around in the system."

You didn't know what that meant.

"She never graduated high school—dropped out and married at sixteen instead. She divorced soon after. But she had curves to die for and was a ringleader of attention, so when she started acting, she made it big. Then, whatd'ya know. She became a sex symbol."

You almost asked what a sex symbol was, but the way your mother finally looked down to stare at you, as if she was remembering something she didn't have, kept you quiet.

A sigh. "Marilyn was beautiful."

You concentrated on the way your mother said beautiful and tried to understand it.

She finished, "You know, I looked just like her at sixteen." Gauzy.

Two boys off to the side, holding Chinese finger traps they just got, begged their mom for more quarters. She dropped what they wanted in their palms, eager to please them, and yelled to have fun as they ran back to the games, quickly lost in the lights and sounds.

The man at the counter shouted, "Next!"

You watched your mother's lips peel like ripe fruit. They curled just slightly, but enough to make it clear the prize *she* wanted. He was middle-aged with a piercing in one ear, and he wagged his finger. It was unclear if he wagged it at your tickets or you.

"Men liked me too. I could've been a star, but I chose not to," she said flatly.

You took a step forward. The prize-giver asked if you were the lucky lady, and you nodded. You stood on your tiptoes and put your winnings on the counter. You pointed to the poster of Marilyn behind him. You said, "I want that." Pristine.

As he reached behind him, he asked if you liked her. You told him yes. He asked if you thought she was pretty, and you said yes again. He said you might have your own poster too one day, because you were prettier.

He easily cupped your smooth palm, fitting the rolled-up poster into your hand before your mother smacked you clean on your wrist and told you no, you would not be getting it. She gripped the collar of your dress, pulling it so tight that it felt snug against your throat. You were dragged from the counter. She hissed, "Why the Hell did you do that?"

You heard children's cries all around you.

You coughed, "What?"

Lights around the games and prizes shattered. Flashes like fractures broke the dark.

She said, "I saw the way you looked at him." She said, "And you touched him. You did it on purpose." One of her sleeves fell lower on her shoulder when she leaned down, eye-level with you.

You swore you didn't do any of that. You had just asked for the poster, but your mother thought you were lying, smacked your fleshy cheek so it stung anyway, and said there'd be no prizes. You needed to get your ass in the car.

The man with the flimsy poster still on the counter did not look at you when he smiled at the next little girl.

Your mother let go of your neck. She walked out the front door, letting it slam in the metal frame behind her. Its noise lost in the other ruckus.

Before you left, you looked at Marilyn one last time. Buckled knees pressed hard together, hopeless hands against the rising white dress, and a vacant jewelry shop, consumed by shadows, close behind. She was harrowing, porcelain, lovely.

All-consuming, painful. And, like your mother said, she was beautiful, sure, but you realized what attracted you most was her loneliness.

You wondered which poster child Marilyn was: sick, suffering, or ideal. You would never ask because you promised, but if you ever learned the answer, you crossed your fingers and silently swore you wouldn't tell anyone. You would keep her secret. You would keep it close. You didn't want to leave Marilyn behind.

PRETTY THINGS

JENNY'S BEDROOM WALLPAPER WAS THE color of coffee stains and hot pink roses, and she had pinned-up pictures of the girls she hated with devil horns markered on them. The lava lamp on her nightstand terrariumed a golden-sunrise blob in the glass enclosure. She had a *Dirty Dancing* poster hanging by a few strips of masking tape above her headboard. There were silky throw pillows on her bed.

Her mom came into her room to give us two juice boxes, and to tell us to turn the music down. Jenny whined that it was practically still her birthday, so her mom said fine, but we'd have to turn it off in a half hour. I went to punch the tiny yellow straw into my box and accidentally missed the hole, nicking my knuckle instead.

Before her mom left, she looked straight at me and said, "Madeline, I've never told you this before, but you've got a beautiful name."

Then when her mom shut the door, Jenny turned her radio up louder and said, "Ugh. My mom's such a loser."

We were sitting on her bed, going through a pile of her birthday gifts and chewing on candy cigarettes.

She said, "Too bad you couldn't come to my party."

When her mom had first planned it, Jenny told me I wasn't allowed. Her mom made it family-only Jenny had said. She threw a stuffed toy monster, a *Ghostbusters* poster, and a Mad Scientist lab kit onto the floor beside her bed and told me, "I didn't ask for any of this junk." She put another candy cigarette between her lips.

She continued, "But at least I got a hundred dollars."

I told her that was enough to buy a new stereo.

"I know. I might buy that, if I don't get a collection of nail polish and a Bonne Belle makeup kit instead. I think if I get some new dresses in colors to match too, that could be really pretty."

"There are so many other things you could get."

"I guess." Then she chewed on her cigarette. "I could get more candy if I had fifteen more dollars." She finished off her cigarette and swallowed it.

Jenny could get more candy without fifteen more dollars; she just wanted to remind me that I owed her. She was known to hold grudges and kept track of things like that.

She'd been lending me lunch money for three weeks, and even though I'd never asked her for it to start, the total she'd given me was up to fifteen dollars at that point. She had just started handing me the cash before we entered the lunch room, and, since I needed it, I took it, but she always expected it back later.

Her mom packed her a lunch every day. Lunchables, Capri Sun, and fruit snacks, so she didn't realize that the cheesy mac and savory meatloaf that those lunch ladies made only cost ninety cents and not the dollar she was giving me. I'd started a nice collection of dimes in the mini zipper pocket of my KangaRoos shoes. That way no one knew I had a savings. I wanted to get a necklace like Ma's—a thin, gold chain she always wore.

I told Jenny, Sure. More candy'd be nice.

She looked at me like I was hopeless and told me she'd be back. She was going to use the bathroom. She said I had permission to turn the music up if I wanted, and when she returned, we could finish off the cigarettes.

Her dresser was straight across from the foot of her bed. It was short enough that I could see the top of it from where I sat. She had a strawberry candle from Bath and Body Works, and a Beanie Baby that could have been a cat or a bear but I wasn't sure from where I sat. There was a mood ring that looked black, and a tube of dollar store mascara, even though she was twelve and I'd heard her mom tell her no makeup until she was fourteen. On the dresser's last bit of empty space was a ceramic purple pig the size of a tennis shoe. I grabbed the pig and almost dropped the cold and slippery thing as I did it. Luckily I didn't.

I'd heard one time that the only way to get the money out of a piggy bank was by smashing it, but this was the first time I'd ever even held one, so I didn't know if that was true. I wanted to see if I could release some money another way.

Jenny was lazy. She did not push her bills in deep, and with the pig's tiny eyes gawking at me, its mouth curled upwards like a little ribbon, I pinched my fingers against the top slit and tried to catch any bills near the surface with my bitten nails.

I heard Jenny's mom yell something, although I wasn't sure what. The Madonna album playing was loud, even without me turning it up.

I turned the bank upside down, making the pig's smile a dramatic frown, because I hoped any coins in there might provide a pressure that could push the bills closer to where I needed them. I knew that if Jenny had recently gotten a hundred dollars, it must be closest to the top.

I shook it, trying to do it light enough to minimize any noise, and then the corner of a bill finally emerged. It reached out just enough for me to pull it free with a few other bills she had pushed in with it too.

I heard Jenny yell to her mom that we'd turn off the music when we were done. I put the bank back on the dresser. Her mom said she had to be done now. I glanced at the bills in my lap. Jenny whined nooo. I counted a ten and two fives. Jenny came back to her room, slamming the door so loud and hard that her mom yelled something unclear, and I jumped in my spot on the bed.

She told me her mom spoils everything.

I remember saying to her, "Yeah, moms can do that."

She looked at the cash on my lap.

"This is for you," I said.

She shrugged like thanks. She was shorter than me, so she had to lean even further to reach her bank, and then she squished the bills up small so she could push them hard into the pig.

The next day, the lady from social services dropped a new kid off at our house. Ma and Dad were so excited that they nearly hugged the snot out of the little girl. She had wiry hair slicked back into two uneven French braids that didn't look all that French. She had a little necklace with a plastic *I* hanging from it, and wore denim overalls. She held a garbage bag of stuff. She couldn't have been more than six years old then, and I think she was seven when we returned her. I'm not even sure of her real name.

I remember Ma waving off the lady who delivered her though, and the minute that lady said bye to us and shut the front door, Dad looked over the girl's paperwork and told her that we'd call her Caroline. I guess she looked kind of like a Caroline, but that poor kid didn't agree and started crying, tears streaking her cheeks and snot in her hands. Ma rubbed her back kind of rough and told her we had a treat in the kitchen for her. I didn't know what treat she was talking about since we didn't normally have treats in the house. As they walked in the other direction, Dad reminded them that they needed to say prayer first.

A few weeks later, Ma came home from grocery shopping with plastic bags that were full to the brim and hanging from her arms, and a fistful of scratch offs that she yelled about to Dad. He came out of the kitchen with a grin on his face, his big Chiclets teeth visible even beneath his metal scrubby mustache. Ma told him it was time, so my parents sat down at the kitchen table covered in coupon papers. Dad handed Ma a nickel, and they both went to work, scratching off our future.

I honestly don't know how much they won, but I know we didn't hit the jackpot that day.

Dad pounded the table with his fist, threw his nickel against the dirty wall, and went to his bedroom to watch a rerun of *M*A*S*H*. Ma loudly opened cupboards and drawers and started making some mashed potatoes for dinner.

On Thursday nights I'd go to Jenny's after school because her mom wasn't home. She had bridge club or something. I'd walk around the outside of their house, through the small backyard, and Jenny would let me in the back door so the neighbors didn't see. She said the neighbors were too nosy for their own good around there.

I told Jenny about the new credit cards I knew my parents had recently gotten.

"I don't think it's a big deal," she said above Madonna's 'Take a Bow' coming from her stereo.

"Really?"

"Yeah, I think it's cool." She added, "You guys could buy anything you want that way." The pile of junk she got for her birthday was still unopened in her bedroom corner.

I said, "But I don't think they belong to my parents." I had found the new cards sitting on the kitchen counter. They had the name Isabella printed on them. Pretty.

"Who is Isabella?" Jenny asked. She laid back on her bed so her hair was hanging down the side and she ran a sparkly Wet brush through it.

"That's the thing. I don't know."

Then Jenny said, "Well, you're rich enough to pay me back now at least. Aren't you?"

I told her that's not really how credit cards worked.

Jenny had still been lending me cash for lunch, and the extra dimes I'd collected weren't nearly enough to buy a necklace yet.

"When Ma gives me some cash, sure." Which wasn't a lie. I hadn't seen any of the money we'd suddenly gotten. I mean, it was credit after all.

Jenny sat up and looked outside her window at the dark. She told me I should probably leave before her mom got home, or we might both get in trouble, but she'd see me at lunch tomorrow. She asked if I'd be going to Homecoming next week because, if I was, I could join her and her friends if I'd like. I told her no, maybe next time.

On my way out, I passed her living room where I saw a porcelain doll on top of the entertainment center. Spotless skin, almond eyes, and a dress made of lace. All she needed was a halo and she'd look like an angel. I took her down, and the plastic-hair smell of a Barbie doll overwhelmed me. Tucked safely in my arm, I took her and walked out the front door.

Dad came home late the next day, which got Ma all riled up. She'd made some frozen Mrs. T's Pierogis that had been sitting out on the counter for an hour. We whined about our hunger as we stared at them, but Ma told us we had to wait for Dad. It was her way of punishing him, I know, because when he finally got home, he'd have to deal with our fury. But when Dad found her in the kitchen and handed her a black box, she couldn't help but squeal. Our cries were irrelevant.

The box had a new necklace, and it looked way more expensive than the one she usually wore. It had five, red, teardrop-shaped jewels, maybe rubies, spaced evenly apart in a semi-circle shaped row. They were connected by a string of diamonds. She said it was a statement piece and she hooked it around her neck, holding the two ends of the necklace together with one hand and her hair up with the other, waiting expectantly for Dad to clasp it shut. He did. For days I watched her stand in front of that bathroom mirror, stroking the jewels, turning different ways to try and catch some light. That first night she got it, Dad kissed her on the cheek and told her she'd never looked more beautiful. She told him she believed it. She said she'd never felt more like it either. Ma tossed the pierogies in the trash can and made a two-finger whistle. She yelled to the house that we were going out to eat, which didn't happen often.

I decided that I didn't hate Caroline. Life actually got a little better with her around.

Caroline had been with us for about eight months by then. She had thrown hours-long tantrums the first week, but after Ma had some sort of private conversation with her behind the closed bedroom door, she was mostly fine. Ma never did tell us what she said to the girl.

Caroline didn't talk to anyone in the family much, except to lie. There was one time I heard my sister tell her about a few things that made Dad really upset, and one of those things included being late from school. If you were late coming home, there was no way to make him happy. Then I heard Caroline tell Dad one day when she was late that she helped a teacher clean her classroom after school. She said she wiped down the chalkboards, swept the floor, and took out the trash. Dad told her that was very sweet of her and let her off the hook. I knew what a bunch of crap that was though. Her school left a message on our machine the week before that said she'd have detention for biting a kid while they were in line for recess. The school didn't know why she did it and suggested we talk to her. I had deleted that message so our parents never knew. I guess she walked home from school the day they kept her there.

Sometimes I saw her steal things, too, like a pair of pink sunglasses from Ma's purse or the fake-gold lighter from Dad's nightstand. She wasn't exactly sneaky about it—wasn't silent. Didn't hide. She would walk right up to the thing she wanted and take it, which is how I noticed the time she stole my black tattoo choker necklace. Joke was on her—I had never even worn it. I'd stolen it from Jenny myself, and since it wasn't even worth anything, I let her keep it.

I'm not sure where she learned these habits from, if she came to us with them, or got them from us, but Caroline was always looking for something she couldn't have.

Ma was having one of her moments where she touched each of her necklace's jewels in her reflection. That day, she'd painted her lips a red that matched the jewels. Her dirty blonde hair, as short as shag, was curled a little, and she'd blushed her plump cheeks too. That must have been the last bit of lipstick she had because the empty tube sat next to the pink seashell soap holder on the bathroom counter. Instead of holding soap though, the dish had her old, delicate necklace in it. She started keeping the soap in the counter's top drawer, and when we finished using it, we'd put the soaking wet piece back in there. Some sort of slimy mildew started coating everything.

I stood right outside the door, close enough to lean in, but far enough to not scare Ma.

"Hey," I said.

She jumped a little. Her reflection waving funny in the mirror that was a little warped.

"Hi, honey."

"Can I get some money for some new clothes?"

She kept her hand on her necklace but turned a little to look at me. "You know your dad and I are going out tonight," she said. "But I'll give you what's leftover and you can go to the mall tomorrow."

She looked at herself one last time, as if saying goodbye, and then walked past me. Once she was gone, I snatched her necklace.

A few weeks later, Dad gave Caroline back to the system. I don't know the details, just that it took a lot of paperwork because he complained about it for days. I heard him tell Ma that it shouldn't be that difficult. They were standing in the kitchen near the tiny, open window while Ma smoked her cigarette. Dad said that the state knew she was damaged, and it's not like she was really theirs, anyway. I heard Ma tell him that they *did* ask for her, and this shows how it can be hard to want things sometimes because giving things back isn't always easy.

The next day Jenny and I were walking to history class.

"Here, I've got some of that money for you. I'll finally get you the rest soon." I handed her back all the dimes I'd been collecting.

She looked at me funny. "Thanks."

Then she put the change in her pockets like it didn't mean anything to her, and when she realized the noise they were making, she scooped them back out, and then I watched her drop some in the trash can we passed.

"That's a nice necklace," she said. I guess she noticed my ma's chain, hanging underneath my shirt.

We walked into class as the bell rang and Mr. Williams was writing on the board. In big, capital letters it read: Roman Empire.

Jenny and I sat down as Mr. Williams said, "The Roman Empire—a republic that formed alliances and went on conquests, and in only a few years grew into something big. It spanned Europe, North Africa, and parts of Asia, and fought in major battles to gain power." He pointed to a colorful map. "The Roman Empire mixed sophistication and brutality to get out on top."

Nicole and Megan started giggling in front of us. Mr. Williams turned to stare straight at them and the giggling stopped. Jenny pulled out a notebook and started writing something down.

Mr. Williams called on Adam in the back and asked him what he knew about the Roman Empire. Adam said nothing, and Nicole started doing some fake sign language to Megan, who just made some dumb face back.

Mr. Williams continued his lecture. "Trust in its reliability and strength."

Jenny finished writing, quietly ripped the page out of her notebook, and folded it up. She handed it to me, with my name written in pink highlighter on the front.

Mr. Williams interrupted himself, saying, "Madeline, what's that bright thing you've got in your hands?"

I watched Jenny go unnoticed by him as she reached for Nicole's purse hanging off the back of the chair in front of her. Jenny hooked her pinky around the temple of Nicole's cat-eye sunglasses that dangled from a purse pocket and silently pulled them out, placing them in her lap.

Without even opening the note, I handed it to him. Jenny's note was a distraction never meant for me.

The nosy neighbors told Jenny's mom that I'd been over, and that I tried leaving the house with no one knowing, so I wasn't allowed back there. That meant that on Thursday nights, instead of sneaking to that side of town with Jenny and her loud music, I'd go sit on the interstate overpass, listening to the cars roar down below, and watch all the birds fly overhead instead.

On one of those nights, I thought about Jenny's response to my parents' credit card fraud. *You guys could buy anything you want.* I wondered, could we? Before they sent Caroline back, Ma bought her a keychain with a little purple geode. Caroline carried it everywhere even though she had no keys. I'd watch her pick hard at the gems, sometimes so hard that she'd pull one loose. I knew that if she kept doing it, she'd have none left. I didn't tell her that though. Instead I watched her destroy it.

With the credit cards my parents had, that was what she got.

Pretty things are easy to want—nail polish, sunglasses, necklaces. The clothes we wrap around our bodies. The faces we paint on ourselves. They help us hide the things we find ugly and hope nobody else will see.

People thought my name Madeline was pretty too. Mothers, strangers, and little girls said so, but I never knew what to make of that comment. Ma once said, "You were the prettiest thing I ever saw the first time I held you," but I never thought I fit my name.

Then, it was like life unfolded in front of me right there in that moment, and I understood it like a formula. Money buys pretty things. People want pretty things. If people don't have money, then they steal. I watched Caroline steal, Jenny steal, my parents steal—even I stole. People thought my name was pretty, which only meant one thing.

One of the birds above me left the flock that had just flown past and landed on the railing of the overpass. It must have needed a break. I watched it for a while, sitting there. I bet no one had named the bird. How did it think of itself? Another bird flew by, accidentally dropping a piece of bread, and the first bird snatched it up so quickly that it flew off without getting caught.

I said, Madeline. Mad-el-eye-n. Mad-elynn. Mahd-ellen. I rolled it around my tongue, tasted it in different ways, and I wanted it gone. I didn't want a pretty name. I knew what it meant to be a pretty thing. I'd watched enough pretty things get taken, after all.

The billboard a hundred feet away had an advertisement for a local bank. An illustrated colosseum covered the sign from edge to edge, with a warrior and his six-pack abs in the center. It looked like the face of the Roman Empire, and see,

Mr. Williams said, "Trust in its reliability and strength."

I was a fourteen-year-old girl. I wanted a new name, but I didn't want to regret it, and

Ma said, "I had to name you something pretty."

when you choose a name, you choose whatever you're interested in the most at that moment. What that means is that, if you're naming yourself, it's still not even about you, but

Jenny said, "Yeah, you can buy whatever you want. Think about how great that is."

the things that are less important.

So I knew that even if I didn't want my name to be Madeline, I didn't want it to be whatever I was interested in at that time either. If I wanted my name to be anything more than Emma, like from the Spice Girls, or Cindy, like Crawford, then I couldn't think too hard about it. In fact, I couldn't think about it at all, because, if I'm being honest, I probably would've wanted something pretty. So without thinking, I decided right then and there what I would be called.

New birds flew past in perfect V shapes over the horizon and into the seedy dark. Birds I'd never seen before. Birds with no names. I, on the other hand, a girl stuck on the overpass, had two names. A dead one, and a new one.

Roman.

And there was nothing pretty about it.

WILL WORK FOR SHOES

1. MANOLO BLAHNIKS

Tom, the man sitting across from me, says orgasms are all the same for men, so I tell him they aren't for women—there's a big range. Then I bend beneath the table and adjust the gold pendant on my black suede kitten heel to straighten it out. When I sit back up, I watch Tom look me up and down, well, what he can see, anyway, with half of me under the table. I begin to imagine what he's thinking of me. I don't tell him that part though. I smile at him and wink, hoping my mascara doesn't leave inky freckles below my eyes. He told me he likes an assertive woman before, so I ask him how much longer till we leave the restaurant. He says soon, he just wants to finish his old fashioned first, and then he'll give me the best night of my life. I let a soft laugh escape. I tap my feet, I mean the hard bottoms of my strappy heels, against the tiled floor, and let him think that he's right. I will always let him think he's at the top of my orgasmic range if that's what he wants, even if the reality is that he's something far more mediocre. Tom flags the waitress over and asks her for a carryout box and I catch him wink at her. With a small strut, she walks away, and I wonder what *her* best orgasm's been. If she ever felt so good she had to scream. If Terry could top hers.

2. VALENTINOS

I've never dreamt of my future husband and mother-in-law cooking Thanksgiving dinner together, but Bobby has asked me to join him and his family for that event as his pretend fiancée. He adds that, also, they will all be drunk before we get there, with an uncle who's not racist but says the colored folk are taking over the neighborhood. So I lay out the ground rules quickly when I tell him sure, but only if he takes me out to three more dinners than usual at, like, that really nice glass restaurant on the top floor of that skyscraper downtown. He doesn't like my conditions, but if he doesn't accept them, he'll be eating the marshmallow sweet potatoes his cousin made by himself at the kid's table because his whole family, he tells me, won't upgrade him until he finds himself a woman. Of course I don't ask him what they'll say when he doesn't bring me around again, but who's to say he won't if he can afford it. He tells me to only say *hello* to his cousin's offspring because the kid will ask if we're going to kiss if I say anything more, and while, yes, he wants to kiss me, many times over, before the night is finished, he says he can't pay me enough to make up for doing it in front of the whole gang, so just say hi and move on. He says I should not expect anything more from them than tank tops highlighting cleavage, and blue jean jackets, and shorts or cargo pants with brown, leather belts, and pockets that can hold handguns, but he wants me in something sleek and classy. He's no cosmopolitan himself, but he says he's got a nice polo, and some khakis, so I tell him I'll wear the shoes I have on, which are black, curved, and shine when the light hits them, and he says he's even going to get a new pair of dress shoes himself.

3. YVES SAINT LAURENTS

Nick won't waste time on dinner because he wants more time in bed, but only on Tuesdays because his wife works nights on Tuesdays, and I know this because he invites me over regularly enough. There are family pictures all up in the hallway, and he's said, Sorry, sorry, I have a wife but she's not here, and I swear I'm sorry, I hope this doesn't ruin things—but I never asked. Of course I told him it was fine, because it was, and it wouldn't ruin anything, because it wouldn't. Of course I let him unbuckle the thin, velvet strap of my sandal heel and rub his rough hands around the soft meat of my feet. Of course I still pressed my fingers against his chest, curled my nails into the fabric of his shirt, lifted it above his head and laid against him on the bed. Of course I asked him what he wanted, did what he wanted, told him I loved the tattoos he had on his back. I don't remember most of them, but I do remember one was a barcode between his shoulder blades. He asked if I had any, and though I didn't want to show him either way, he saw that my skin was bare when it was time for him to remove my shirt. He mostly stopped mentioning his wife after that, except he'll sometimes still bring her up as he apologizes for the photos of her hanging right next to us. I've stopped responding to those comments to try and show him it doesn't matter. I buckle my own shoes back up when we're finished and think about another pair I might buy after Nick pays me. I wish he'd stop bringing her up because I'll ignore whatever he wants me to for those new shoes. The last time he had me over, he asked me if I'm married, and I am seriously so sick of him even mentioning marriage. I know he's just sorry and is trying to make conversation, but I can't honestly answer him, or I'd have to tell him that, no, I'm absolutely not married, and then he might ask why, in which case I'd have to tell him the truth—because I'm not interested. Because I know that marriage is the closest thing to dying.

CROSS TO BEAR

THERE WAS A BEER CAN caught between the hood and the windshield of a car I walked past, and a bumper sticker that said *Christians, Consider the Unborn for President*. This was on my way to a bar that sat between a music store named Garage Band, and a smoke shop named Puff Puff Pass, and was as close to the expressway a building could get without being on it. Inside the bar was a group of six women dressed in pink boas and plastic tiaras—already sick from alcohol for a bachelorette party, at least ten men watching the Friday night football game on the tiny television above the bar, and three men in hunting jackets but not sitting together. Other women curled into other men. People. People. People. A bartender sprayed whipped cream on a man's chest behind the counter, and a woman, straddling his lap, used her tongue to clean him up. She grimaced. It was difficult to tell which person in there might be the owner of the vehicle outside. I sat at the bar stool in front of the register and before I could even think about who I might meet, a sentinel man in a jade-colored work shirt and a golden cross hanging from his neck like a noose dropped his hand onto the counter in front of me. He leaned in on his elbow, his breath so close I could smell the devil on it. He asked for my name and called me honey in the meantime. I shook my head, clearly told him I was waiting for someone, and he smiled. He fucking smiled. He said his name was Jerry, and he asked if he could buy me a drink. Glasses clanked against the things they touched all around the bar counter like Jerry's hand. I told him I don't drink, which was a lie, but I don't drink alcohol from strangers. He told me about where he grew up, and no matter how many ways I turned away, said no thank you, and looked at my watch expectantly, Jerry still asked where I was from and then wanted to tell me about how he was with his poker buddies over on the other side of the bar. I didn't bother looking. He finally said good night and walked back to his friends, leaving me to myself, the bar's clutter, the racket, the mess. Then a waiter dropped some fruity margarita off in front of me and told me it was courtesy of the man across the bar. I couldn't see him through the crowd, but I felt him smile. A woman from the bachelorette party wobbled past me in a dress shorter than her fingertips and heels at least six inches tall—I imagined her pain. I stood up immediately, stopping her with my hand on her shoulder, and asked if she liked fruity drinks, but before she said anything, I told her it was from a man, that way, and pointed somewhere behind me. I didn't even wait for her answer but placed the glass in her palm, forcing her fingers to curl around it so it didn't fall, and I walked out the front door. Down the sidewalk on the way to my car was the man in my peripheral, his gold cross gleaming underneath the towering streetlamp. He dropped into the driver's side of the vehicle with the bumper sticker, and some other woman folded into the passenger seat. The roar of his engine starting. A loud bass escaping the space of his rolled down window. A coarse whistle squealing from his tires. A woman inside the bar with a drink she never asked for. Who wants this?

GIRLS MAKE MISTAKES

"THERE WAS A BOY I kissed once, my first kiss, thirteen, in his mother's basement, circled by a group of mutual friends."

"I bet you were embarrassed, because didn't you still like his friend?"

CENTERFOLD WANNABE

IT TOOK THREE WEEKS, BUT Luca finally apologized for skipping out on the baseball bleachers, which meant he was really apologizing for not pulling you in with the back of your head and force-feeding you a sloppy kiss, even though you had really wanted it—especially after that dream you had about hooking up in the mall bathroom. He told you his brother couldn't wait after school that day, and his brother was his ride home, so that's why he didn't make it to the bleachers. When you asked him why he ignored you in the lunchroom the next day, he said he didn't see you. When you wanted to ask why he never went out of his way to find you after that, you didn't. You accepted his apology instead.

"Can I ask you something?" Luca looked at your lips like they were a series finale and asked if you'd give him some pictures instead. He said he'd been thinking about you for weeks.

You couldn't say yeah fast enough.

He said, You know, pictures of you. Naked.

You said, Yeah, I get it.

He added, You'll get some pictures too. You know, after. He pinky promised.

You asked him when he wanted them, and he said, The sooner, the better.

You had one photo left on your yellow Kodak disposable camera, so you knew how important accuracy would be under this circumstance. Like, the lighting, the angle, and the way you were made-up needed to be perfect. You spent all of fifth and sixth hour planning, drawing naked women in your notebook. An arched back against a white mattress. A firm bust, powerful in front of a mirror. You couldn't pick which pose you liked best. Dominic and Mario laughed about something behind you. You didn't like them, so you covered your drawings with your hand so they couldn't see. You almost asked Collin, the nice kid who sat next to you, which one he preferred, but then the bell rang and Collin handed Gloria a note. Gloria wears white slips as dresses, pink plastic butterfly clips in her hair, and red coffin nails longer than your lips. You grabbed your notebook and left.

At home, there was no mother, a paper bag on the counter, and a stapled note that said DINNER. DON'T STARVE. You considered opening the bag, but then pinched the fat on your belly instead. You felt the flesh soften between your fingers. You tossed dinner in the trash.

You looked at the naked woman in your room. In the photo, she is lying with one leg bent to her bellybutton, one hand across her chest and holding a tit, and the other hand bent back to grab her butt cheek. She is something to be desired.

She is the centerfold in the adult magazine you took from an estate sale two years ago. Looking for cheap jewelry, you wandered around the nicknacks and old coats in the strangers' living room. You overheard someone saying that the house was built in the fifties and the owners had been the house's only occupants. It sounded as if the couple had died. A cardboard box next to a record collection was full of magazines, and you put the one on top inside your winter coat before you left without saying bye to the person running the place.

The magazine said the woman's name was Cassandra, and you only took her out of her hiding spot under your bed on special occasions.

You liked her caramel-blonde hair and how it looked like a man grabbed her by it. You appreciated the dismembered shadows and sun-bleached, spotty light she was bathed in, like someone opened the lid, just a little, to a memory box in which she'd been concealed. But as you stared at something this perfect, you questioned why you agreed to do this.

In the photo, Cassandra's mouth is open like she is astonished or surprised or excited. Her eyes look dead.

You did your best to position your limbs in a way that mirrored hers. You bent and grabbed and squished. You opened your mouth painfully. You tried to be both innocent and alluring, exactly like she was, but couldn't figure out how.

Then, you realized there would be no way to pose like that while you held a camera simultaneously—not if both your hands groped onto the round, sweaty hills of your butt and boobs.

In front of the full-length mirror propped against the wall, you got down on your hands and knees, mouth open, tongue hanging, and with the little camera underneath you, between you, angled up, you snapped a reflection of yourself. That was it. That was the last one.

Dominic says he wants sweet *or* salty. He doesn't really want anything in-between. You hear this from somewhere behind you. Mario tells Dominic that sweet and salty bars taste like shit anyway. He adds, "Things that have two flavors come across as confusing. They are harder to enjoy." He says it like he means it.

You hear Dominic over your algebra teacher when he says, "You know, that makes me think of this one time we developed some photos of a dude's breakfast bars. Like, they were different photos taken on different days, but the same goddamn thing every time. Like, seriously, an oatmeal breakfast bar."

"Weird, man."

"Yeah."

Dominic works at a local drugstore. He's not old enough to do half the important things, so he mostly watches someone else do them. He talks about what he sees all the time.

The boys start to whisper, but not quietly enough. Dominic has seen some other weird shit too. Like what? Like naked people.

It seems like Mario is unsure if he's supposed to be intrigued, turned on, or disgusted. He says, Is that weird? Sometimes.

You don't draw naked women today. Instead, you write the name Luca as many times as you can on a single page in your notebook. You haven't spoken to him since he asked you for photos earlier this week. You're still waiting on the call that your photos are ready for pick up.

You hear Dominic say that they developed another weird roll yesterday. He's not sure who dropped it off, but there were pictures of overgrown toenails and coral-colored lips.

You stop writing.

Mario chuckles and says that's weird.

Dominic continues describing some void that might have been up a skirt.

Your breath becomes pulpy, and you choke on the thick, pasty texture.

Mario tells him if it's that hard to tell, it probably isn't. Up a skirt, that is. It may have been the inside of a purse for all he knows.

"Maybe. Guess what though?" Dominic asks. He says that the weirdest photo on the roll was actually of a naked girl who looked like a mutt. On her hands and knees, with her tongue hanging out like she's panting.

Your breath is something moist and beaten, something you can't get out.

Dominic tells Mario about how he's not allowed to process film yet, but the other guy who works there does. You find out that the other guy's name is Lars, and he's in his early twenties, so sometimes he bends the rules.

"We're not allowed to develop nudes or photos with sex in them."

"That makes sense."

"I don't think so if they've given them to us to develop—it's lame. But we're supposed to give the negatives back to the owner, unless they're doing something illegal in the photo, and then we gotta call the cops."

Mario asks if Dominic's ever had to do that.

"Nah, bro. Not me. And there's times Lars should have." But he'll usually develop them anyway and take them home instead. "This time, she's mine. I took her home."

You think you hear Mario tell him, Dude, that's sick.

Sick like cool?

Your teacher has sat down at his desk to grade papers. He doesn't look up. You hear some shuffling, and Dominic's softer voice lets you know that the boys have leaned into each other.

Mario says, "That's a bit weird though, don't you think?" He coughs. "I mean, that's like, a girl's personal stuff."

You start digging your pen into circles so hard in your notebook that the page becomes a big black pit. Luca's name has been completely marred.

Dominic says, "Why not? I deserve a keepsake." He says the job's shitty and doesn't pay enough.

Kids around you talk, sharpen pencils, and write down answers like nothing's wrong. There is noise, but your strained ears still manage to hear the fringes of, "*And*, I know it's hard to tell"—Dominic's voice falls to an even softer hush—"but I think the girl in the photo is her."

You're sure he's pointing at your back.

He finishes, "So it's like a trophy."

You try to spit up the shapeless mass caught in your throat, but find that nothing comes out. Breathless, you circle your pen so hard into your paper that you rip a hole into the blackness you've created.

You understand now that the face Cassandra made was one of appalment.

You wait for what they will say next. You know that whatever it is, no one will bat an eye because it's coming from boys. That's how things work.

Mario says, "You know that's child porn though, right?"

PRETENDING TO BE HAPPY

WE HAD BEEN HITCHHIKING, LOOKING for some kind of flimsy summer happiness, when I flagged down the car about to drive past us. Joyce wore fishnets, and I had on my Yves Saint Laurent pumps that made me nice and tall. The driver slowed down, staring at first, but then he winked. I tapped Joyce and told her, Look—he's watching us. He smiled a little, and she couldn't help but giggle. I told her, Aw, Joyce, stop it. She brought lips, red, so she put them on without even looking in a mirror. She said that this was where two women could find the happiness we were looking for.

The man rolled down his window and reached out his arm. He waved us over, so we walked to the side of the road where he had pulled up. Joyce asked me if she looked okay. She started petting her hair and I told her, Yeah, she looked good. Not like the time we went to an all-you-can-eat buffet and she put crab legs in a big bag hanging from her shoulder, her hair all frizzy and knotted up in one of those tie-dyed scrunchies.

I knocked on the passenger side window so the driver's friend rolled it down. He smiled a gummy smile, his hair short like an Air Force man, and he asked how us ladies were doing. Joyce went to say we're good, but the man interrupted her and said he'd like to make our day better. I blushed.

He waved his finger at me to get in the car. I looked to the side at Joyce, and she nodded her head reassuringly, so I did what he wanted. His friend got out to sit with Joyce in the backseat, and the driver got out to help me into the front, holding my hand as I sat down. He was tall, but when I stood, we were almost the same height with my heels. He said his name was Ken. I don't remember his friend's name. He asked if we'd like to go to the drive-in and Joyce said sure. We were looking for a good time. On the way there, we passed the corner gas station with the clothes and shoes donation bin. It made me think about that time me and Joyce climbed in there late at night and found some nice sweaters we took. I don't think anyone knew. They were donations anyway. Then Ken said we've gotta stop for gas first, so he pulled into that same gas station and parked his car next to a pump. Ken said he was hungry so he left his friend to fill the tank, and me and him sat in the McDonald's across from the station.

I saw him reach into his pocket and pull out a ten, which I thought was nice because women don't get pockets on most of their clothes. The black and brown miniskirt I was wearing was too tight. He told me to get whatever I wanted, so I ordered a double cheeseburger and a large Coke.

Joyce and the friend never joined us inside, so when we returned to the car, we found them in the back seats, legs tangled and bent, kissing sloppy. The friend had red lipstick residue all around his mouth like some sort of clown.

Ken and I shut our doors, and I leaned in to kiss him. It was nice, except the front seats had those cupholders between us so the leaning wasn't easy. He pushed my hair behind my ears, and I made sure not to kiss too far off his lips because I figured he didn't want lipstick all over his chin.

Finally, some guy who worked the gas station knocked on our windows and shouted through the glass that we had to leave. We said, yeah, sure, we were, but Joyce snuck another kiss first and her man didn't even wipe the lipstick off his face before we finally did drive off.

The sun started to set, but we made it to the drive-in soon enough. I don't know what movie played—we didn't watch it. The car next to us had foggy windows, so I know the couple inside it didn't watch the movie either. No one took their clothes off or anything though.

At the end of the show, Ken asked for my number. I didn't usually give my number to the guys we had fun hitchhiking with, but I made an exception for him. He told me he recently got an apartment and he liked my style. He said it needed a woman's touch, and who was I to argue with that?

The drive back to Joyce's house was deep dark, but underneath the streetlamps I could tell that a girl who was walking downtown wore flip flops and a bathrobe. She walked aimlessly, but girls like to do that before they get lost, and so easily, too. We passed the girl and we passed a gas station with a sign that said All Cigarettes On Sale. Joyce asked if I wanted to go to a bowling alley but it was really late so I said no. We kissed the men one last time for the night. We went home.

Ken invited me over Wednesday, and since I didn't have anything else going on that night I told him sure. When I buzzed up to his place, he came down to open the door and bring me up. His apartment was small but nice enough. He had a couch and La-Z-Boy and a little coffee table in front of a big box TV. He asked if I wanted wine or a beer and then he got me a beer from his otherwise pretty empty fridge, which was fine because I'd have drunk whatever he gave me anyway.

We were sitting there, talking, sometimes kissing, sometimes laughing, and watching some old black and white movie that was on one of the few channels he had. I figured he didn't bother paying for cable. He was wearing a short sleeve shirt that night so I saw the lizard tattoo on his bicep for the first time. I told him I always wanted a tattoo and he said, Yeah? I said Yeah. He told me he could give me one. I asked him, Really? He said sure, so we made plans the next week for him to give me a tattoo.

I told Joyce about it the next day. She said I should think about it, but if I really wanted it, she'd support me. I thanked her because I was gonna do it regardless. She sighed. She had her hair in a knot on top of her head, held together with a scrunchy again. A little worse than her buffet hair, but no one else was going to see her that night. Later in the conversation, I remember saying, Hey, why do so many women read romance novels? She said, Yeah, men don't do it. We decided that women just want a happy ending. They want to know someone can love them, but real life proves them wrong every time. I guess those books give them something to dream about.

Back at Ken's apartment next week there was a sign taped to the front door that said *NOW CLOSED*. I buzzed up anyway and Ken came down. He said his neighbor was sick of strangers or something and we laughed. He placed his hand on my lower back when I walked up his stairs because he lived on the second floor.

I asked him how long he'd been doing this for and he said a few years. He knew an artist who did it and taught him some tricks of the trade on the side. I was surprised he had a machine at home—never met anyone else who had something like that—but I didn't ask him why. I did ask to see his work though and he said he had no pictures, but he showed me some drawings he had in a sketchbook and they looked nice. There was a tiger with real fine fur and a good shadow that hid part of his face. The stripes looked like chains at first glance before I realized what they were, which was silly because I should have known better. I told him it was a nice tiger, but he corrected me. It's a tigress.

He had me lie on his couch, which was comfortable enough, but I had to lie face down so he could access my bare back. Sometimes I couldn't breathe, but maybe that was okay because sometimes I wanted to yell and instead I bit the cushion.

He asked what I wanted. I told him to surprise me. What the tattoo was didn't really matter, in my opinion. He said okay, and that he knew exactly what he wanted to do. I smiled. He kissed me hard before he told me to put my face back down.

Some few hours later he finished, and when we went in front of the bathroom mirror, me still shirtless and holding my tits with my hands, we tried to get it so I could see behind me. My back faced the wall mirror, and he gave me some woman's little hand mirror to hold up above my head, trying to see the reflection of my behind. When I finally got the mirror's angle right, I saw the tattoo. It was a devil in a woman's costume, or maybe the body of a woman on the devil, I couldn't be certain.

I told him I loved it.

I showed it to Joyce, and she asked what it was supposed to be. Like, is the woman eating the devil? No, I don't think so.

He put it in a spot that got mostly covered by shirts, unless I was in a cutoff top, so it wasn't hard to hide it if I wanted. I don't recall how frequently I showed it off.

I got together with Ken a few more times, but like how it is with most men, a few times was as long as it lasted. I never decorated his place. Joyce didn't hear from the friend again either, which she said she was fine with, but I knew that wasn't true. She said a lot of things she didn't mean, or meant things she didn't say, when pretending to be happy. Like, she never said it, but I was sure she disapproved of my tattoo from Ken—but what did she expect from me?

We finally went to the bowling alley.

Another day we were walking down the road to the theater. Joyce had chopped her hair into a pin-straight pixie cut that morning. My hair was the same old perm. A car pulled up next to us, and although we weren't meaning to hitchhike, we went up to it anyway. The man had a worn windbreaker and a goofy smile. He introduced himself as Ollie Gunther and asked what we were doing, walking by ourselves. Then he asked if we had any responsibilities. Joyce told him no. She meant not right then. In a rather flirty way, he asked if we'd like any. Joyce looked at me expectantly, like this could be an adventure, maybe something happy. The man unlocked the door. She got in the car without my blessing, and even though I knew better, I followed. I guess I wanted something to dream about too.

BLOODY MARY

I WAS AT RING AROUND the Rosie's because I'm poor, but Rosie's is a lucky place you see. I've been working at Rosie's since I was fourteen, and now at twenty-two, I've got seven regulars. I pay special attention to two though because they like to tip me well.

The first is Theo. An old man who doesn't make food for himself ever because he comes to the restaurant for dinner every night. I don't think he's ever bothered switching up his order, at least not the entire time I've known him, so everyone on staff knows it by heart, except the new girl who can't even remember to bring silverware to the tables.

Theo likes to smack my butt. He did it again not too long ago, and while it normally doesn't surprise me, it did that time. I dropped the forks I was carrying and they smashed against the ground. Clank clank. To save face, I bit my lip, and before letting the flesh slip from between my teeth, I leaned down to grab the forks, glanced back at the old man, and then stood up. He smacked me once more, and that time the slap made a loud noise. My right hand, which was not holding any forks, grabbed his wrist hard and nearly pulled him off the bench he was sitting on.

I was lucky he liked to play it rough, because he sure made me angry sometimes.

"Your lipstick's smeared." He revealed a gapped-tooth smile that I knew too well and slipped me two twenties.

I licked my lips how he liked it and stepped on his toes. He let out a yelp as I walked away, but alas, luck was on both our sides that night because he was lucky I didn't stab his eye out with a dirty fork.

There is a claw machine at Rosie's, up near the front door, where the snotty kids like to rub their fingers all over the buttons, even when they haven't put any goddamn money in the machine, and then pound it like that will make the metal claw move, scoop down to rescue their prize.

One time a kid had his own luck, smacked the button really hard and the claw started up like it had a life of its own, squeaking across the machine. The snot-rag hadn't put any money in, but there was some weird juice left over from the last one who played it, so it moved until it hit the end of the track and dropped, its bony, metal fingers wrapping around the head of a gray, stuffed platypus with a busted eye. The fingers clamped, dragging the creature upward until the machine just stopped, ran out of energy, and left the stuffed animal hanging by its neck.

I walk past the machine to get to the bathroom. The platypus is still hanging. As I push the door open, my second regular walks in and gives me a wink. Name's Andrew and he's closer in age to me. I'd guess mid-twenties. I nod back but am too busy thinking about how I have to piss that I don't have time for pleasantries. The bathroom stinks. I think it's the hostess's job to clean it, sure ain't mine. I grab the last of the paper towel before going into a stall and spend the entire time I'm peeing thinking about Andrew and how the hostess probably sat him at a table in my section. I wipe myself with the paper towel, don't bother washing my hands since there is no paper towel left, and wipe my fingers against my apron. They are dry though—it's not like my hands are soaking wet from pissing.

Andrew is at the wooden table closest to the front, facing the bathroom door. Gives me a wave when I walk out. I wink at him and lick my lips a little. Taste my cherry lipstick so I give them another lick.

I walk over and get, "How're ya doing, pretty lady?"

I promise he's not southern, or a cowboy. He's pretty suburban, if you ask me. The kinda guy who works some mildly corporate job in a black button up. Not too uptight like some of those people, but he knows how to work his way around a business. I think he's just trying to flirt. I take my pen from my bun, letting loose some stray hairs so they hang in my eyes, and tell him I am great. Never been better. Especially now that he walked in the door. I think I winked too. Men like attention like that.

I ask if he's getting something new that night and he tells me no. Says he likes to know what he is getting himself into.

I put my pen back in my hair and walk away without making a sound and he lets me. He doesn't say a thing.

Whatever Andrew is, he's got some money because he always leaves a nice tip. That's why I give him special attention. It's also why I assume what I do about his work. I don't know much about that life, growing up on Ramen and spotty electricity, but my brother Dean did. I'm not sure *exactly* what Dean ended up doing, but he was some kind of credit guy working on Wall Street. He used to talk about leaving for New York when we were young, but I always thought Tess and I were gonna go with him. We were going to stick together, you know? I dreamed of that life too, but I guess that wasn't a part of his plan. Us sisters got left behind in a no-name city on the outskirts of Detroit.

Dean got a degree in finance when I was in the tenth grade, and on a night Tess and I were piercing our ears out on the back deck, Dean booked a flight and went off to the big city. Mom said he cried a little when he told her to pass it on that he said goodbye, but I know that's not true.

He used to be cool when we were young, a little bit of a bad boy in that he'd sneak out the window and go up to the gas station to smoke cigarettes with friends. Sometimes he'd invite me and, even though I was younger, he'd let me taste the smoke. He'd say, "Go on Katie, catch it in your mouth," and I liked the way we played games.

Then he was a Patrick Bateman—still the bad boy, but dressed nicer and throwing money around like he was important. Brought home a girlfriend one Thanksgiving who wouldn't stop talking about her brother's abduction, and then he made us all tell her we were thankful for her—it was so weird. Then she still came around the house even after they broke up, and especially after he died. Now she brings her new boyfriend with her, another yuppie.

One time my brother told me that the best piece of advice he ever got was that whatever you do, make sure to give it one-hundred percent, but he was saying this to me while I sat on the ground unclogging hair from the vacuum cleaner and he stood almost six feet above me. On a visit home, back from New York, he didn't think he needed to take his shoes off in the house anymore. They were fancy dress shoes, some kind he never owned before leaving. I couldn't even tell you the brand.

When we found out Dean had died, I wasn't surprised. Bad-boy shit on Wall Street is normal, but can get you into trouble if you don't watch it. I guess our bad boy didn't watch it. They found him in the East River with some sedatives in his blood and a few bricks in his pockets. His skin was bloated and loose from being under water a few days. I almost asked to see him, but knew Tess might throw up even at the thought so I didn't.

Dean Thompson wasn't the first man on Wall Street to die a suspicious death. I'm sure he won't be the last. We found out because his girlfriend called us, crying through the phone. Her cries sounded like accidents.

I bring Andrew his plate, a quarter pounder with extra cheddar and everything else that comes on it. A side of fries and cheesy broccoli—I don't ask, never do, don't want any customers to think I'm judging them, even if I am.

We're surrounded by old license plates and street signs. I'm pretty sure the owner stole most of them and hung them up like trophies. He never dusts, I think the hostess is supposed to do that too, so when people get seated here, they end up sneezing a lot. I try to avoid serving anyone in this section if I can.

Andrew tells me about how he saw a movie that made him think of me. He thinks I'd like it. The main character is an alien who zips herself into the bodies of beautiful people. I laugh at him and tell him I don't watch movies. He asks me why not. It's one thing to admit you don't watch movies, and it's another to talk about how you're roped into watching your niece whenever you're at home instead. Tess is a bartender, works later nights than I do, and likes it I think, except our mom is always asking us why we can't be more like Dean. More successful. It's a weird way of saying she'd like us at the bottom of a river. I just tell Andrew that I will watch it when I have the time. That's what I usually tell people because it's easier.

I walk past a family of four—mom's a bitch, dad's a prick, and two little brats. One of my socks rolled down my ankle earlier and bratty kid number one laughs and doesn't say quietly that I'm not dressed right. I'm sure Bitch is proud because she laughs too. She says, also not quietly, "Yes, you're right, but we don't say that in front of people. She can't help it," and by that, I don't think she means that I'm on my feet all day and don't have time to pull my sock back up. I'm grateful that they're not my table, but feel bad for the new girl waiting on them because I already know they won't tip. They probably leave a note that says Jesus Loves You on the receipt instead.

Andrew's a little messy and got some kind of stain down the front of his shirt while I was away, so I walk up behind him, place my hand on his shoulder and start rubbing some dish soap in slow circles on his chest. I've served him long enough that this seems okay.

"When do you get off?" is the first thing he asks me. I notice a few crumbs that the busboy never wiped off. Using my bare hand I go ahead and swipe them to the floor, leaning my cleavage into his shoulder while I respond with, "Sorry—let me get that for you."

"I know you guys close in a half hour. Ten?" he says while he stares at my tits.

"Then why'd you ask?" I use my fingernail to scratch at my lip. I go ahead and pat his table to let him know I'm leaving. I make sure to step so my ass wiggles when I head back to the kitchen before I look back over my shoulder at him.

It's ten-forty because we never close on time and I'm on top of Andrew in the driver's seat of his car. It's the first time we've ever done anything like this. I've known him three years I guess but you'd think it was longer than that, and in a typa way that wasn't just serving him burgers, with how he's sucking my lips. He said he doesn't care that I'm wearing lipstick. Said he likes it. I guess some of that Rosie luck has rubbed off on him.

He grabs my waist, pinching the skin, and pulls me in closer to him like he can't breathe. I hear his keys rattle in his pocket and the steering wheel is pressing hard into my bare ass. We're parked under a street lamp in the parking lot and even though most of the cars are gone, I know that whoever's gotta come back to the last one there will get a full view.

"Put your mouth on my neck," I tell him. I know that men like it when you tell them what to do.

"Yes, ma'am."

"I want your tongue against my skin."

Andrew grabs my hair and pulls my head back so he has more surface area in front of him to stain wet.

Now he says, "I want you to talk to me." He says this while he's breathless. This is weird, but he gave me a really good tip tonight so I'll say whatever he wants I guess.

"I've been wanting this for years," I say. I haven't, but I'm sure he'll like hearing that.

"Have you?" He's still breathless as I drag red tracks down his shoulder. I took his button up off before we got in the car.

"Mhmm."

"What have you thought about?" He moans, his eyes closed, his head rolled back.

I tell him sucking his dick, but mostly because I don't know what other lie to tell him right now.

My knees start to sweat on the leather seats and make a noise as I shift my weight on his lap. That's when I see Theo walking across the parking lot. He's holding a joint in one hand and dipping his other in his pocket.

I immediately roll across the center console, a few pens in the cupholders ramming into my meaty thighs, and lay my back against the seat. I desperately reach for the lever somewhere on the side, my fingers searching, and then finally lay myself back.

"I want you on top of me."

If Andrew's on top, Theo won't see me and I still want Theo's nice tips too. They say money doesn't make you happy, but I don't think they've ever grown up poor.

Andrew doesn't say anything, but knees me in the crotch when he moves on top and I giggle. When he looks at me funny, I tell him about the time that half the city thought I got a tattoo down there. Someone saw me in a tattoo shop window with the artist's hands between my legs. I laugh again, but this time it's because I know what was really happening. He sees that I don't have a tattoo there, but he also doesn't ask.

He kisses me hard again, biting my tongue, and I think about how I'm never going to watch that movie he suggested.

Andrew's back at Rosie's next week and this time when I hand him his burger, we're next to a bear crossing street sign hung crooked, and he invites me to a strip club.

"It's really great people watching, I swear."

I pull on my lip a little and smear the lipstick around.

"I can't. I've gotta watch Hailey." Hailey's my niece.

He tells me not tonight, but sometime soon. I'll have time to find someone else to watch her.

I leave Andrew to help another customer, a grizzly man with a fuzzy beard, and it's obvious he hasn't shaven in a week. We don't talk the whole time I'm serving him. I bring him his bill and this guy starts speaking to me all the sudden like I'm his therapist. When I say we didn't talk the whole time, I really mean he just said Caesar salad to me and that was it. But now he's telling me about how he had died out there and came back to life and God is telling him He wants to save me. I need to be saved.

I tell the man I really hope he has a nice night.

I think all the time about how Wall Street's a trap. Especially when Dean's ex-girlfriend and her new lover sit at our kitchen table with us since they've come to town. My mom won't listen to me and Tess, says it's completely normal to keep them around even though we know it's not. His ex wears a bra that's too tight, and a skirt that's too short, and I'm not judging when I say this, it's just a fact. You'd think so too if you saw her. I asked Dean, the Christmas before he died, what he saw in her. He told me I wouldn't understand. I asked him why and he said, "Look at you. You're a waitress at some kind of dive-restaurant in Detroit. What do you know?" She has diamond earrings that match three of her rings.

Somehow I end up at the strip club. It's one near Eight Mile and it's not even classy, but I guess that's the best kinda place to people watch. I didn't tell Andrew that I stopped watching people when I realized how ugly they could be, but I did tell him I'd drive myself.

I pull into the busted parking lot and notice first the missing shingles next to the sign that advertises high caliber women. I notice second the paper sign that just says *Open* hanging from the door.

Andrew spots me pulling in and he's grinning, confidently. I can't tell if he's attractive or nervous. He approaches my car. I see him think about it first, the way his eyebrow dips before he decides to wrap my back with his arm. He almost kisses me but lets that thought pass. I notice that he's wearing Buffs and smells of a very clean cologne—one I can't name.

"I'm glad you came." Andrew says this to me as we walk in together. "You'll have a good time."

I think about when Dean went to a strip club, when he first turned twenty-one and then after getting his job in New York. He said he took a bunch of singles with him the second time.

Once in high school, our bad boy took Dad's car. From my understanding, no one ever found out except me and that's because Dean brought me with him. We took I-75 to downtown, to some seedy party store, and the man at the counter sold us some beer, even without ID. I made sure no one found out. When Dad spotted the leaking tire because of the rusty nail Dean drove over in that parking lot, I told Dad *he* drove over a nail when he picked me up from school earlier that week. Told him I hadn't said anything because I didn't realize it would cause a problem. I was just in high school, right? I couldn't have known better. It took Dad a few weeks to save money for a new tire and he thought I was stupid as shit after that, but Dean got off clean.

I'd never been to a strip club, but Andrew swore I'd love it. Now we've got a table near the stage and a waitress with long locs asks if I want to order anything. The prices are ridiculous, so I hand her a sticky menu back and say no thanks. If I wanted piss-poor alcohol for that price, I'd go to the grocery store and just get more of it. Andrew hadn't said anything, but she comes back with a glass. I'm not sure what it is but it smells sour. She's got red, coffin-shaped nails wrapped around the drink she hands him, and then he orders a Bloody Mary.

"Already?" I look down at what he still has in his hands.

"No, it's for you. You'll like it."

I'm about to tell him that I don't want it, but the waitress is quick, almost spills it in my lap as I start to say no, so I guess I'll have to take it.

The first woman walks on the stage, wide hips and saggy tits. Her bikini barely covers her nipples let alone supports anything, and she takes tiny steps in her seven-inch-tall heels. She gets to the end of the stage and sits on her ass. Andrew tells me to watch the men, and women, gathered around with dirty singles laced between their fingers. To engage the crowd, she moves differently than a normal woman would, but she doesn't do any tricks on the pole, or even dance for that matter.

Andrew leans into me, pressing his hand against the top of mine and tells me to watch less of the stripper and more of the people surrounding her on the floor. Those people are helpless.

So I watch them, like zoo animals, from a distance, and the sad thing about it is how they don't even know. A near-naked woman has power, and her power means everyone else has blinders on. Nothing exists except what is in front of them.

Andrew nudges me, then points to one man sitting next to the stage but positioned behind the stripper. He watches as she bends forward for someone to stick some singles in her strap. He has a full view of her ass. "He's doing it right."

"Why's that?"

He ignores my question, says, "She's doing better."

Her panties are still on but full of hanging money and she hasn't even done anything. Seriously, no tricks. The lights above her flash and light the faces of each person below her, highlighting the nameless people.

I look at Andrew next to me. He is mildly interested in the scene unfolding in front of him.

"You look the way I imagine my brother did before he died."

He glances over at me, stares at my lips. Probably at some sweaty lipstick rubbed down my chin, thinking about how I look the way a lion looks when devouring his prey. He reaches over and rubs it off my face. A red print left on his thumb.

"How did he die?"

"He drowned next to Wall Street."

"Wall Street's not that powerful."

Tell that to my brother.

Some man near the back dressed in black, as black as the shadows in there, starts emptying the trash and no one pays him any attention. You don't have to agree with me, but I think that dude deserves to be making as much as my brother did. This guy probably didn't leave his family behind either.

Andrew's out here talking about how Wall Street's not that powerful as we watch the waitress pocket a five-dollar bill she slipped from a man in the front row when he wasn't looking. Men don't seem very lucky here. A thick cloud of smoke lingers around us and, I kid you not, I swallow a ring like old times.

"You ever think about getting rich?" I ask.

"Every day," he says. He bites his lip like he knows what he's doing.

"Money changes people," I say.

"Money makes you powerful."

I shake my head. No, it is a certain type of job that does, or a certain identity, but aren't those the same thing? Andrew's arms are leaning back against his chair, his elbows bent. So casual.

I don't know how he does it, but he knows what I am thinking. He says, "You can get power doing anything. Watch those women," as he points to a new woman on stage, heavy, with small tits, and a bunch of facial piercings that the party lights reflect off of. "They aren't walking around in suits, living out in Beverly Hills."

Two new men push their way to the front of the crowd and wag the woman down with their bent index fingers. One who looks Eastern European, with a buzz cut, grabs her chin and almost makes her and her eight-inch heels wobble over. He gets really close, nose to nose, then shoves a thick wad of wrinkled cash in her bra while he fingers her nipple. The most impressive part is that through all this, she doesn't even flinch. When he finishes, she winks and stands back up which makes the other guy call her down too.

"Have you ever thought of doing something like that?"

I shake my head.

"You could." Andrew looks me up and down.

I stare him in the face. "You know, I was happy when my brother died," I say, like that's some sort of appropriate response. I think back to the images I made up of him held under the water, bits of skin floating away.

"You don't have to be like him."

And I know he's right.

"But think about a life with more money."

And I do. I think about a life with more money. How that might look. No more leftover customer dinners eaten behind the counters in the kitchen at Rosie's. Regular AC in the hot, gummy summers. A Christmas gift to give Hailey.

I watch the waitress set another Bloody Mary down on a table up front. I realize I haven't even touched mine.

The music's loud. A third woman has joined the stage, knee-high nylons hooked up to her panties. She's only out there a few seconds before she looks at me. I see something in her eyes. Not sadness.

"I'd support you," he kinda whispers to me, loud enough so I can hear, though.

I don't reply.

"I have an in."

I give him a side-eye.

The third woman on stage spins to face us so I can see a big number seven on the thong's triangle hiding her vag. The three women touch each other, running spiny fingers up legs and down backs, in each other's mouths. More cash gets thrown on the stage in waves.

Andrew's hand lands on my knee.

I hear a song that I don't know but somehow recognize.

I watch a couple at the table on our left and they're making out. Andrew's hand still rubs my knee. I think of his lips earlier that week and the way they felt on my skin. Andrew's hand starts to move a little higher up my leg. Lucky Number Seven is kneeling, legs spread open. Number Two is untying the strings holding bitty pieces of fabric over Number One's nipples. Andrew wraps his arm around my shoulders. The women walk all over bills beneath their heels. The man changing trash cans is gone, I didn't notice him leave. The lights highlight curves.

"Do you see that woman?" I hear Andrew say.

I didn't but then I did. Sitting on the other side of the stage, she's cute, but clearly not a stripper. Too many clothes. Some middle-aged man, nearly hunchback and balding, walks over to her and passes her a couple dollars. She shakes her head, which seems to mean she's not an employee, but the man pets her hand to tell her it's okay. She is still a trophy, I guess.

We sit in silence for five more minutes, the strippers' heels clanking as one by one they leave the stage and someone new replaces them. A carousel of fantasies. Someone's escape. Andrew asks me what I think. He's a peripheral noise. Across the way, I notice a wrinkled face I recognize. A bird nose, white fuzz on the chin—it's Theo. *What luck.* If there's anything I know about Theo, it's that his attendance is loyal.

The song I might have known is over. A new set of women I don't recognize is on stage. Andrew's in my ear saying something about my red lips. About how Bloody Mary could be a good stage name for me.

I lift my untouched highball glass, ice rattling its insides, and finally take a sip. It's got a kick to it—*spicy*. I do like it. A smudge of my red lipstick, like incarnadine blood, stains the edge.

"Sure," I say to him.

BLOODY MARY

A woman's thin strap on her heel is snapped, held
together with a hair tie.
Its owner starts parading.
The table is sticky. Bits of napkin are stuck.
This whole evening is a wildly improbable event.
I can't smell anything except sweat and cheap perfume.
But that's what luck is.
Lights split the space in fragments.
We're all victims of our circumstances.

So yeah, I repeat.
Sure.

After all, I think, I always serve people.

DON'T BOTHER

MY JEANS WERE UNZIPPED WHEN the cop pulled me over, but it was a happy mistake.

Late at night, traffic lights sprinting in my peripherals. I saw his siren first, I mean heard it, saw his flashers. I knew there'd be trouble.

My pants were already unzipped. That was an accident. I didn't do it for him.

But because my zipper was down, the first thing he didn't catch was me texting on my phone. The second thing he didn't catch was the cocaine under my back seat.

He was tall enough, sandpaper scruff along his jaw, and a triangular nose. His badge was perfect-straight.

"Miss."

He tried to look me in the eyes.

"Yes? …I'm sorry."

Still trying to look me in the eyes. My hands were on my waistline.

"Miss," and then, "I shouldn't be doing this," sitting in my passenger seat. He put his hands on my panties.

I didn't think anything of it, didn't tell him to stop, it's not my job to tell him to stop. After all, we make bad decisions around here. So I let him. Told him it's okay. I undressed myself like a carnival show, some kind of celebration. He watched.

It didn't take long. We were on the side of the expressway, his flashers still flashing, headlights whizzing by. My phone buzzing under his heavy breathing, sister asking where the coke's at. I'd get back to her later. The cop kissed me goodbye. He told me no ticket this time. I almost spit.

I zipped my pants up. *The New York Times* said unbuttoned jeans are a fashion statement now-a-days, but I was only full from supper. I started the ignition, turned the left-hand blinker on to let everyone know I was leaving the shoulder, rejoined traffic, and drove off without a ticket.

Because a man won't even really look. If he'd bothered, he'd have found what he was actually looking for.

WHAT HINTS MEAN

WE SPOKE TWICE AFTER OUR second date and I tried to contact him twice after that but, somewhere in my adult life, later than it should have been I'll admit, I learned that if someone doesn't respond anymore, then I should take the hint. It was on my couch that I sent him a text which, consequently, ended up being the last text I'd send him since he never responded to it. It said something about how I hoped he had a great time on his trip home, because he wasn't from Michigan like me but he was from Florida and he visited home for Christmas. The text also said that I looked forward to hearing from him because I, at the very least, did hope that I'd hear from him. Even if I wasn't sure about him, about us, because he was uncomfortably shorter than I and into unusual art and clicked his teeth when he was thinking, I liked the idea of it. Besides, he seemed really into me which I liked because I've been dating for three years and that's three years way too long, if you ask me. I sent the text on a Monday night because I figured at that point he must be back from his trip. Two days went by and I heard nothing back. Then a week. After four weeks of not hearing from him despite my reaching out, I realized that a month had gone by since our last date and that apparently it hadn't gone as well as I thought. Either that or his plane from Florida crashed, but it was much more likely he wasn't interested. We'd gone to the bar where neither of us drank that night, to watch a band that neither of us had heard of, but before the band went on, we laughed at the couple sitting next to us. We made up a life story for our waiter. We talked about music we actually prefer and we told each other secrets about things I won't ever admit to anyone again. Then we listened to the band we didn't know, which was okay. Afterwards, we went on a walk in the city that had just been covered in a thin layer of snow even though I knew it would soon be more because Michigan layers snow on top of snow until no one can stand it. Being from Florida, he didn't know that yet. I like people watching, live music, and walks so I thought the date went well but maybe he didn't. Maybe he was unhappy that at the end of date two I hadn't leaned in to kiss him or my hand hadn't slipped against his so that we could hold each other. Maybe he was unhappy that I hadn't told him he was beautiful yet. Maybe there's more to relationships than finding someone who spends hours talking with you like they care. With all the dates I've been on, I've realized that never seems to be enough, and now that I have so many hints I've had to take over the years that I have a collection, I'm starting to feel like, at some point, this many hints should turn into an answer. Maybe then it would be easy for me to slip my palm against someone else's.

PERIOD SEX

IT'S THE END OF FIFTH hour aerobics class and we're all changing out of our gym uniforms in the locker room when Gwen stands on a bench so she's taller than the busted red lockers behind her and says, "Period sex is the best." All the girls in class, wearing sweaty t-shirts and knee-high gym socks, curve around her like a congregation in front of the pulpit. Gwen's fourteen, I think, and I would have never guessed she'd had sex before. I had assumed that all of us were virgins—except maybe Lindsey, but she's always out of school, getting in trouble, anyway.

Mary has mascara smeared under her eyes from sweat. She says, "I mean… I've had sex before, but never on my period."

Then more girls in cheer shorts rolled two times at the elastic band begin admitting to their own rendezvous with boys from school, but they all agree that they wouldn't think to add the red stuff to the mix.

Gwen, pulling her scrunchie off so her hair falls all over her bare shoulders, confesses she's been doing it since she was twelve. She's learned it's just easier when she's dripping with blood.

The boys have started leaving their own locker room adjacent to ours, with their shoes squeaking against the gym floor, making noises so loud we can hear them from where we are.

Call me naïve, but I'm with the majority of the girls here. Who wants sex when they're bloodied?

Leah, whose arms are crossed, her scarlet nails spotted against the bleached t-shirt covering the flab of her triceps, asks the question we're all wondering.

"Why?"

Still towering above us, in her faded blue jeans with a hole on one thigh and a lacey black bra she's already changed into, Gwen declares it is slicker.

I see Janelle look at her differently, like Gwen's an evangelist preacher. Something incredibly powerful and gruesomely predatory. Tara winces, probably at the thought of drainage down her leg and all over her boyfriend's crotch. She says, "You're risking a lot."

I will never forget what Tara says next.

"I mean, the boys will think you're impure."

Gwen lifts her arms and then bends them, pulling a fitted white t-shirt down over her head. She shrugs. She reaches her fingers up to spin one of four earrings nailed into that ear. Her hair's dyed a copper penny color.

She says, "It feels better that way."

Janelle goes back to staring at Gwen like she's a victim.

The bell shrills and we all jump and scatter like a bunch of stray cats. Janelle waits for Gwen to hop off the bench and they walk out together. Gwen's shirt is so tight you can see the band of her bra through the back of it.

I've watched enough horror movies and crime scene shows to know how disgusting blood can be. All the forms it can take. I think of blood from open wounds and shredded skin on dismembered body parts. Blood soaked in the oatmeal texture of vomit. Blood smashed against a wall behind a gunshot victim. I think of the blood her body rejects each month and wonder why she insists on slathering herself in it. Like, I really want to puke at the idea of Gwen having sex with blood.

But then I can't help but think about doing, you know, *it*, with a faceless boy myself while I bleed beneath him. I surprisingly let myself go in this vision, unbothered by the way his body uses me like a tool, then leaves me there when he's done. I'm all spattered and stained, like *I'm* the victim, though I know I'm not. I really don't think what's supposed to be pleasure should be unsettling like this, so I guess I take solace in the fact that he's also been marked by my gore.

CRUSHING

YOU WERE SIXTEEN, BUT LUCKY if you looked fifteen on a good day, even if you wished you were twenty-one on all the days. You wore a fingertip-length skirt and no underwear on a summer afternoon when the sun was highest and the sweat crowned your forehead. With a fistful of quarters, you walked up Ten Mile Road to the gas station for a Red Faygo. You hoped you'd see Will on the way, who was seventeen and going to be the next Tony Hawk. He'd do a kickflip on his skateboard, and was working up to a three-sixty flip. You wanted nothing more than to swallow this boy whole, to taste the salt of his skin pressed against your teeth, to be so close you could bite him open. Something about wounding him with nothing more than your open mouth felt sexy to you. Maybe that's because you'd been taught that sexy is a woman splayed out, arms and legs stretched wide, eager to be devoured by men, your whole life. Will was not a woman, but he could be that same type of centerpiece for you, even if only in your dreams.

You felt the serrated edges of the quarters against the soft girl flesh of your fingers. You hummed something and rubbed droplets off your forehead, slicking your free palm with sweat. Cars drove past. Rush. Rush. A squeaky tire. Your hum softened under the weight of the metal. Then up ahead you saw him, Will, with a flat-billed cap on backwards. You watched him skate to the edge of the curb before stopping himself from falling over. You had almost hoped he'd keep going. Hoped he'd feel the rush one feels when faced with uncertainty, even if the probable crash is obvious. And with all those cars around, so many eyes passing by, no one would even notice. If they did, they might only stare in hopes to see the pool of blood.

You were watching Will without the blood though. He turned around, and then a shrilling honk from somewhere on the road shattered your thoughts. Your shoulders jumped, you dropped a quarter, and you watched a middle-aged man, older than your mother, wave to you as he passed. Before disappearing, the man honked his horn three more times, loud and hurried, and your heart raced. You knelt down to pick up your quarter, your bare knees scraping against the sidewalk. You noticed Will across the street still practicing tricks. The honk didn't faze him.

Not taking your eyes off the road, you counted three more heads of men turn to follow your figure as they passed.

IT DOESN'T TAKE MUCH

WHAT I'VE LEARNED ON THIS trip: America loves sex, fireworks, and Jesus.

Daria's in the driver's seat of her tan, two-door, '90s Honda Accord with her window rolled down and arm hanging out of it. She's letting it flap against the wind. She's got Boston's 'More Than a Feeling' blasting from the radio so loud that you can't even hear her singing along to it, except for when she's really out of tune on some of those long notes. She's been singing like this for the whole state of Tennessee and part of Georgia.

"Daria, did you hear about those strippers who showed up to Taco Bell?"

She doesn't hear me.

We've been driving since one in the afternoon. Her cassette player's kind of wonky and the speakers play a little fuzzy but she's ran through Styx, Journey, Queen, and ZZ Top however many times you can in nine hours.

"I guess some guy sent them there," I say like she heard me the first time. "He paid them money to go to Taco Bell." The story aired on the local news this morning.

The billboard we just passed on the expressway that says [$tripper$ - Exit 164] is all black with a white font and white silhouette of a very voluptuous woman. You can't see her face. I don't know if Daria didn't notice the sign, chose to ignore it, or just didn't say anything about it, but it's hard to miss when the sky gets swept by a long line of these signs on our route. There were at least four others we passed, noting that the strip club opens at noon and has been featured on an episode of *Jerry Springer*.

We run over what looks like a raccoon, some coarse, stripey fur, that's already been road-killed, smashed pretty good, but she keeps going. Who knows how many others will run over the pummeled, decomposing flesh next.

"Who?" She asks, her sweaty fingers turning the dial to the left so the sound falls way down like the crash of a waterfall. She'd know if she had been listening.

"What did they even do there?" I answer instead.

Her eyes flicker up towards her bangs as she thinks about the possibilities. Chapstick smeared over her lazy lips.

I know that different people have different reasons for stripping, but a lot of the strippers around us come from the poor part of town where they're desperate for money, which is sometimes a consequence of growing up broken. A different news channel did an exposé on the number of strippers who are survivors of childhood sexual abuse a few weeks ago. It's a pretty big number.

Daria finally answers me and says, "My guess is that they didn't do anything because they were getting paid anyway—"

"—Or they ran with the joke and made a big scene. Do you think the scene was with the employees or the customers?" I ask.

"You think it was a joke?"

The sun is turned down like the dial. It's dark as a skunk out here in the night as we drive along this empty stretch of highway. We pass another billboard and I'm thinking it's going to be another sign about strippers, but it's not. It's another black sign, but with yellow and red font this time and it's advertising [Fireworks!—Exit 121].

It's not even that time of the year.

Daria's question must be rhetorical because not only does she not answer me, but she also doesn't seem to care that I never answer her. She's tapping her fingernails against the steering wheel to the beat she's got in her head. It's 'Wheel in the Sky' now and I mostly only know this because she's played it six times already.

One time, during our freshman year, she told me about how there was a guy who paid her to kiss him in the mall bathroom when she was twelve. I remember telling her that was weird, and then I found out the guy was seventeen, so I told her it was wrong, but she said it felt good to take his money. My first kiss didn't happen 'til I was sixteen and while I didn't end up dating the guy, at least I wanted to.

Daria lives with her grandmother. Well, her grandmother, her grandmother's boyfriend, and her four brothers, but it's her grandmother's house. She tells everyone that where she lives now is where she's from. I think she was born in Des Moines, but it's not really my business to ask. It's pretty clear she doesn't like to talk about where she's from or where she's been. To be honest, she doesn't like to talk much about where she's going either. All I know's that we're heading to Tampa on account of the UFO sighting she heard about last week. She called me up, even though we aren't as close these days, to say we ought to go. I asked her if we really had to chase it, but I knew the answer.

She's singing about running down dusty roads. She stops herself and looks back over to me. Her brown bob is a tornado, pushed around by gusts of wind. She looks at me and the middle part of her lips begins to open, but I turn my head and look out my own rolled-down, passenger-side window. The wind snaps in my face but it doesn't seem as bad as the wind whipping in the driver's side.

"Have you ever wanted to go to California?"

There aren't too many lights out here. A lot of corn fields, I think, but I can't really see anything specific in the sea of dark. It's us, the three hundred feet of pavement we can see in front of us, and the billboards. Except I see a crow swoosh in front of the headlights so swiftly that he somehow misses our crashing into him. So close.

I completely disregard the fact that I know California's number one in UFO sightings when I tell her no, I've never really cared to go to California. It seems too hot there, over-crowded, and dirty. I think she knows I feel that way. She doesn't say it, but I know she's thinking about how Florida is settling. She probably thinks she's doing this Florida trip for me, even though I would have never suggested we make this trip either. She has to know though if she'd told me to get into the car, we're going to California, I would have agreed to follow her along on that trip too.

We pass another billboard, this time it's lit up, like the fireworks are crashing down on top of it.

"I'm going to try and go there next time, I think." Her spidery fingers clutch the steering wheel harder as she keeps her eyes pinned on the asphalt. Her hands remind me of a daddy longlegs but I'll never tell her that on account of it being rude and because she never really had a dad and I think it's a little sensitive for her.

"Okay." I mean, I really don't have anything else to say.

Daria's been obsessed with aliens for years now. I'm not sure when it started, but I know the obsession's gotten bigger since her grandmother started hooking up with that man, I think his name is Jack, and Daria's had to do more with caring for her brothers. She never even liked her brothers but now she's mostly their mom. She's told me about how the youngest'll leave all his Hot Wheels out, or maybe it's his Legos, I don't know, they're all the same to me, although I know that's not true for people with kids 'cause Daria makes it clear that one is different than the other, even though I'm not sure how because she ends up stepping on both. But the kid will leave all his pointy toys out on the floor and you'll never see Daria in a pair of cute flip-flops ever because of it. Her grandma's up at the corner bar, Slippery Slope, most evenings—that's where she met her man, Jared maybe? I think that's why Daria spends so much time at home with the boys.

"Look for an exit, will ya?"

"Sure."

"I don't think I've seen one for a few miles."

We pass another sign on the right advertising a store with fireworks, and fifteen seconds later we pass one on the left with information about another strip club, different than the one featured on *Jerry Springer* though. Both of them are advertising exits a ways away still.

"You need to use the bathroom or something?"

Daria's bob wags back and forth. She glances down at her dash all lit up like it's a city fair. "Nah, we're running low on gas."

"How low?"

She says that she can't really tell. The lights mean nothing and she doesn't know the last time they worked but it was probably before the car was hers—she got it pretty cheap off of some used car lot. Sometimes when the light comes on, she's got a lot of time before it actually runs out. Sometimes when the light comes on, there's not a ton of time left. It's sort of like a game of Russian Roulette.

The next billboard we pass is a solid white with the picture of Mary, the Virgin Mary, dressed in a blue robe, holding onto the infant Jesus. In large font it says [Choose Life: Pray Pray Pray] and there is no exit listed this time. We had seen another Jesus billboard back near the Tennessee border. That one said that [Jesus is the Answer] and was decorated in a bunch of crosses. That one didn't have an exit either.

Then the car stalls. I've never been in a stalled car before, but it's like Daria took the key right out of her ignition so the car slows down real quick and she's over there cussing. She's banging her fist against the steering wheel, it squeaks, and she lets out a long moan like the way an old door makes a noise when it gets opened real slow.

"That's the quickest it's ever happened."

She's talking about the switch. The switch from a low fuel light to no fuel. She's lost manual steering, so with a big grunt and rough twist of her arms she manages to slightly angle the car toward the right shoulder with the last bit of roll it has. Her tires crunch rocks and pebbles while the car comes to a stop, and that's it. She puts it in park and drops her head back against the seat with a thud.

Maybe, if I'd been a little more excited about this trip, if I'd taken over the responsibilities and let her be a kid for once, tell her we should stop and get gas soon, we'd have filled up a half hour ago and this'd never have happened, but I didn't. I wasn't even thinking about gas. Besides, she knows her car better than I do (which isn't saying much).

Daria steps out onto the asphalt, slamming her door shut extra hard and leaving me inside. She's turned the headlights off, so it's dark except for the thrash of stars above us. You never really notice how some parts of the expressway don't always have streetlamps 'til you need them.

There was a time I heard Daria talking to her grandma about how aliens were our next greatest discovery. That we couldn't be the smartest things out there. Her grandmother lit a Marlboro cigarette and blew an unimpressed whisp of smoke at Daria's face. I was thirteen and sitting at their dining room table that was not in a dining room but at the entrance to their kitchen and covered with months-old magazines and wax candles. I picked one up that was labeled Pumpkin Spice, but it smelt more like the metal utensils at a surgeon's office.

I'm saying this because Daria looks out here now like she did in that moment she had to blow the smoke from Grandma out of her face.

Daria and I met in second grade. That's when her grandma first moved them to the area and she got put in my class. Her hair was long then, not short like it is now, and I was obsessed with it. I'd sit behind her and twirl it in my fingers. I never asked if it was okay… but the strands of her hair twisted so delicately, they felt like the long, hard-spun silk of a spider. I guess it's weird when I think about it now, but it wasn't at the time. I said something to her, and it didn't matter we had nothing in common. We were immediate best friends. Inseparable.

I was an only child, and even though she was busy with her brothers, it wasn't too hard to sneak her out most of the time since no one paid attention. Give me a break, I mean, none of her brothers *died*.

We really liked to go to the convenience store a mile up the road where we'd buy some colored pop. The bricks were sun-faded and some really messy ivy climbed them aggressively. The old tile floor inside was still from the eighties and the wire shelves were lined with expired potato chips and Twinkies. The pop machines were always sticky, but I don't think pop expires, so whatever.

We had just left the house, made it out onto the main road, and she'd been telling me about wiping the youngest boy's puke off her favorite t-shirt. We must've been around fourteen then. She ended up throwing it out, and put on a blue tank top that was too small for her instead. I remember this because the top was mine from a bag of hand-me-downs I gave her that summer.

I didn't see it before I heard it at first, because it came from behind, but the ratchet honks made us both turn to see a red, rusty pickup slowing down behind us. At first, I thought maybe he knew Daria. I asked her if that's what was happening, and she just said, "Monica, let's move faster." I wasn't really in the right kinda shoes for fast moving, some daisy sandals with one strap wrapped around my ankle, but faster we moved. The man wouldn't stop honking though, even though other cars were driving around him, and then he slowed down more to move alongside us.

Daria was freaking out—her lanky fingers were wrapped around my wrist, pulling me forward so hard that I was tripping over my own feet. She never did tell me why she acted that way, but it wasn't too hard to figure out. I didn't blame her for being scared though because I guess we all have demons.

There was a honk, *Come on Monica*, the swoosh of a little car whipping around the truck, *Faster*, a few more honks in a row, my sandal slipping off my foot, the man yelling *Hey there girls!* Daria looking over her shoulder at me, me trying to reach down for my sandal, *Hello! Girls!* Daria's gasp, *Can't you be nicer?*

I could still hear the honks when I pulled away from Daria's hold and quickly grabbed my sandals off my feet. By that point I was getting nervous. I'd seen the way men affected Daria, and I didn't want it happening to me too, so I decided to run. I ran past the fire hydrant, the dentist office on the corner of the next block, and nearly passed the convenience store before I turned down the first side street I reached. The houses were little bungalows with small flower pinwheels and squirrel statues stuck in the front gardens. I kept running till I was out of breath and bent over, hands holding shoes against my wobbly knees, blisters starting on the bottoms of my bare feet. The house I stopped in front of had a pug barking out the front window.

Daria never caught up to me, and she moved her textbooks and jacket out of our locker on Monday. I know it's terrible, but I didn't go out of my way to find her, to ask her what happened, or even to tell her why I did what I did. Don't get me wrong, I've felt guilty all these years, but I don't think talking about what happens to girls matters. We all know.

Every now and then she'll call though, and even though we graduated last year, she'll still ask me to help her escape like before. But now the escapes are bigger than a convenience store. Now it's to travel across the country in search of UFOs.

I put in some elbow grease and eventually jimmy the busted passenger door open. Daria's back is against the driver's side window as she's running fingers through the little bit of hair she has.

"How long do you think it will be till someone drives past and pulls over to help?" I ask.

"Hopefully longer than it takes to kill us."

"I'm not ready to die yet," I say like I'm kidding. Daria doesn't find it funny. After taking a breath, I add, "You know, I don't actually think it was a joke."

She turns to look at me.

"The strippers. I mean, I think the man sending them to Taco Bell thought it was a joke, but I don't think *they* did."

"No?"

"No. The news said he paid them to do it… so they did what they were expected to do, like they have their whole lives. They got in trouble anyway."

And I believe that, I really do, that they were paid to go to Taco Bell, upset because others thought it was a joke, when they were just trying to survive.

Without much sound around us, her swallow is pretty audible, and I'm sure I hear Daria say, "Aren't we all?"

There was a time Daria had told me she thought she might try stripping. Maybe she still thinks about trying it sometimes. Or maybe this road trip was a way to keep herself from becoming a stripper after all. If she did start stripping though, I guess I wouldn't blame her.

I can't see the front of it anymore, but as I stand against the car with Daria, I look back to my left at the Jesus billboard that we passed. I don't know the last time I've been to church, or even when I believed in a god, but I drag a Hail Mary across my chest like I've seen them do on TV. What can it hurt? To my right is the rest of I-75 and the next billboard a mile or so up the road. Even from this distance I can tell that it's another one for fireworks, an explosion of colors against the board, and there's Daria, standing on the asphalt that's bleeding into the sky—running into the jail bars of her escape plan—and then there's me, wondering when this will all be over. My eyes adjust a little to the darkness now that we've burned ourselves into it for a while, but not enough. Everything's still unclear. There's a buzz from some outside critters that I don't recognize, and the heavy sigh of the interstate as two girls sit on its back, or shoulder, or whatever people call it, while we wait.

Daria says, "You know, the Milky Way is over thirteen billion years old, and our solar system is only five billion. We're just a baby. We can't be the only things alive."

And then it comes: a red truck with an American flag decal on the back. It looks like that truck from years before, and even though it was ready to race past, it notices us and slows down, rolling to a rough stop.

She continues talking to me, "But if aliens get to us, it might not even matter. We might be faced with what's called temporal isolation. Like, they might come to us at a time in our history where we can't coexist because we're not advanced enough to understand them."

I can't see inside until the man rolls down his passenger window.

"Think about how many galaxies haven't been born yet. There's a strong chance we might one day be way older than those galaxies and the life on their planets. If we ever meet that life, they probably won't be able to understand us. Trauma is just one big loop."

"Ladies," he grunts. With the way he mutters, I can't tell whether he asks if we're safe, or if we need a lift, or something else. His engine rumbles. Some dust whispers itself off the highway, coating his bumper.

For a minute, I feel like I did when we were younger, like I should run, but I've got nowhere to go, and I promise myself I won't leave Daria this time. She squeezes me when I grab her hand, refusing to look at him as he talks to us, and I get it, but also think this might be our only chance to escape.

I say, "We'd like a ride."

The man leans over to push open the passenger door. I pull Daria into the truck that's far too tall for either of us, and I try to make myself smaller so we both fit in the seat where I'm between her and this man. He asks where to, and I tell him we just need a gas station because we're out of fuel. He chuckles like he knows something we don't. Daria stays silent. I wish I knew what she was thinking, although I may never know—probably won't. The man starts his engine so it revs loudly, and while I'm in-between fireworks, Jesus, and maybe the next stripper, all I can think is that it didn't take too long for someone to pull over after all. But then I realize that in this place, it also doesn't take much to end up like roadkill, blood on the highway.

WE'RE ALL STRANGERS

LATE-NIGHT PRISON RELEASES ARE THE same as death row, thanks to correctional facilities and the gods who run them. I rub my palms rough for warmth against my upper arms and say, "God fucking damn it," as I walk under a streetlamp clustered with moths. It's two in the morning and I'm in a tank top as I leave the prison entrance with nothing but a small wad of cash I might be able to buy a bus ticket with, if I can get to the bus station first.

I hear a man call out to me. He says, "Need a lift?" He's sitting in a fancy car.

I tell him I'm fine. I have a way home.

This is a lie.

He asks if I'm sure. Is there anything I need. Food maybe.

I think about how the hundred bucks I have won't be enough for a ticket, food, and somewhere to sleep, so I tell him food would be nice. One of the dirty moths lands on my hand and I go to smash it, but it flies off instead.

We are inside his car. The seats feel like leather and his center console is clean. He doesn't have wrappers and coffee stains and change in it like the cars of people I know.

The man tells me he'd ask where I'd like to go for food, but there's limited options out here after midnight. He tells me we're going to White Castle. His voice sounds smooth like honey syrup, spread thin on minutes to make them sweet. I scratch the skin on my wrists. I ask him when we're going to get there.

Sitting next to the drive-through menu board they talk out of, he tells me the lobby is closed. "But it's okay, we can just eat in the car." I like his smile. His voice makes me want more. I ask him for his name and he tells me it's Jay.

"Jay. I like that." The words taste synthetic.

Jay orders me whatever I want. I tell him I want three sliders, a large onion ring, and the biggest fry they have. I only expect one of those things but he repeats them all over the intercom. He enunciates the words, and somehow he makes these things sound more delicious than they are.

I decide that Jay is in his thirties. Maybe forties.

I don't notice that he didn't order anything for himself until he hands me the full paper bag.

"Don't worry about me. Eat."

So I reach in and grab a fistful of fries. I notice the radio is silent. Jay asks what I want to put on. I shrug and press the buttons without even knowing except for that I want something.

The salt on my tongue isn't enough. I want more. I eat everything. I tell him I'm thirsty. Jay laughs and rubs my back.

I let him. It's too late to try and fight him and, besides, it feels a little nice. I ask what he's doing out here at this time anyway, and he tells me this happens often. "You ladies get let go in the middle of the night and what are you supposed to do? I can't let you sit outside the facility knowing very well that it's happening."

So you're some kind of volunteer, I ask, and Jay says he guesses you could call it that. Or an angel.

Jay starts driving. "Where are we going?" I say with a full mouth.

He asks if I have a place to stay. He adds, "Come home with me. Let me get you some clothes tomorrow."

That sounds nice.

Street lamps funnel past the car as Jay drives for at least an hour. When we arrive at his place, I don't even pay attention to what the outside of it looks like. Inside his house, I ask Jay for a lighter. He says sure, but watch out. He hands me a lime green plastic one that I immediately roll into a spark. The flame gets larger until I blow it out.

"Get some rest," he says. He points to the couch that has a pillow lying flat against the arm and a throw blanket draped across the back. He adds, "I'll see you in the morning."

There is a gold-looking floor lamp next to the couch. A big screen TV across from it. There are Sports Illustrated magazines and a remote on the coffee table. I take off my pants and pull the thin blanket across my exhausted body.

"What's for breakfast?" I yell down the hall after Jay.

He doesn't respond.

I wake up to the devastating sounds of a semi-truck barreling down the street. With my hands, I cover my eyes from the light coming in the bay window that sits behind the couch, and I smell the leftover grease and salt from last night. Jay is already dressed, in some kind of fitted jeans, a white t-shirt, and Timberlands. He says get up. Let's go. He tells me it's time to get some clothes and I, still without pants at this point, stand up anyway.

The department store he takes me to has a perfume counter and designer handbags that sit on shelves along the walls.

"I don't want any of this," I tell him. I turn away from Jay and look over at the makeup counter where some woman is having her face colored in spring tones. Another woman paints her cheeks with a brush until they look red and shiny like apples.

"Don't worry about it."

"I mean, no. I don't want it. Like, I'm fine with a pair of jeans and a t-shirt. Like, what you're wearing."

He shakes his head.

Yes, I tell him. Yes.

He points at the lingerie. He says, "You've got to get something. What about a nice new pair of panties?"

Why.

He tells me it's a gift. Just get a pair for Christ's sake.

The underwear is black, red, and delicate. It's a size too small, and I pick the next one I see. It's a thong held together by straps and silver metal rings. I walk past Jay and throw it on the conveyor belt moving towards the cashier, and Jay says, "Nice."

In the car again, Jay asks me if I want some coke. He tells me some friends are on their way over to his place and they will bring it with them.

Some guys are kneeling next to the coffee table and smile up at us when Jay and I walk in. One of the guys, with a short, red beard, waves us over. His arm swooshes through the air. He, on the ground, reaches for my leg and grips my thigh. Then I'm kneeling next to the coffee table. I'm not sure if the man has said something or not, but I see what everyone's waiting for. I nod my head. I lower it to the table as if I eat like a dog.

"You enjoy that?" Jay asks.

I laugh. I rub my nose with my fingers and nod my head. I say, "I love it." I add, "Thanks." The man with the red beard points to the next fat line on the table and tells me to have some more. He says, "You're welcome."

And I laugh again. I ask the men where they're from. I tell them I'm from prison. I ask the men what they like to do, like, what are their hobbies. I don't wait for a response. The man with the red beard points to more coke and I shake my head. I shouldn't. He says, "Chase it, baby girl." So what can I do but do it. I touch an arm beside me, and I feel the skin of my stomach with my other hand. I say I missed this. I run my hands through my hair. I say, "Give me more," and the men do. For the next two hours I breathe in, I stand, I give a one-two punch to whichever man's beside me, like I could take him in a fight, and then after fifteen minutes of telling the men I love them, that I'm so glad I met them, I start sweating, rub it off on my jeans, and drop down to my knees again to snort the next line on the table.

Jay rubs my back. He says, "All right, now it's time to pay me back."

I giggle, and sweat from my forehead falls first to my nose and then down again to my lip and I lick it off. I say, "What?"

He goes, "Yeah."

He nods at the guys who grab my shoulder.

I say what.

Jay tells me, "I bought you food, and I gave you that lighter, and I got you some smokin' lingerie. I also gave you that cocaine. Girl, you owe me."

I shake my head. No. No, I didn't ask for any of that stuff.

"I sure didn't offer you that lighter."

Okay, I asked for that, but I'll pay for that and that's it.

"No," Jay says. "I've got a different idea."

I mimic Jay. I say, No. I repeat, No. No, no.

Jay doesn't touch me, but he tells the men I'm theirs. He says, Take her to the bedroom and you can have her for the hour.

Theirs. Theirs. Theirs.

I always belong to someone.

The bearded man has my arm locked behind my back and another one picks my lanky body up effortlessly. I tell them I need more. I tell them let me go. I'm pinned to the bed and Jay shuts the door behind us. He says, "Have fun." He probably imagines my milky skin glowing against the king bed's black sheets. I bet he thinks about strands of hair wrapped across my face, caught in my mouth, wet with tears. He sets a timer on his watch.

My skin is red, a noticeable handprint hugging my upper arm, when I walk into the living room later that evening, after the men have left. The sun is down but there's a floor lamp on, Jay's gorilla feet up in the recliner and some reality show on the television. The lines on the table have been cleared.

My skin feels a size too small and my hair too long and I almost forget to grab my shoes as I walk past Jay, the living room, and coffee table to the front door.

"Where the fuck do you think you're gonna get coke out there?" is the first thing he says to me. He adds, "You'll want more." Jay walks over to me, rubs me on the back, and points to the kitchen where there's a bag of fries and a pile of salt packets. "I got you something."

My head lolls over. My eyelashes petal like wildflowers. I've got a cut on my lip, a smudge of red blood. I almost laugh, but then don't.

"You haven't eaten all day, baby. C'mon." Jay's hand on the bottom of my back. I can't argue with him because he's right.

I sit heavily at the breakfast table in the corner of the small kitchen and exhale audibly before picking up a few fries and placing them in my mouth, one by one, my teeth uncomfortably big around each of them.

Jay sits across from me. He says, "Don't worry. It gets easier."

I rip a small packet of salt open with my fingernails I desperately want to file down.

"One day you won't even think about it."

He adds that one day the whole thing will be warm and smooth, and I'll melt.

I pour the entire salt packet into my mouth. I close my lips. I feel the burn against the cut there.

Jay looks at me. He looks at me in some sort of way I recognize. I try and put a name to it.

He narrows his eyes like fractures and leans in to wipe some salt off my lip with his thumb. I feel crystals fall, and his finger pushes my mouth open, and it rubs against my teeth. It's sweaty, and makes things taste like the low-hanging afterglow of a stretched-out strand of sunshine. I wonder if he'll spoil against my skin.

Animal. That's it. He looks at me like an animal, like the way I've seen barefoot hunters in movies look before capturing their targets.

But who doesn't look at me in that way? Everywhere I go it's the same thing. The world sucks.

Jay promises me some more coke later, once I finish eating whatever meal of the day this is. I don't know, and it probably doesn't matter. He promises me somewhere to stay, he says, "You've got a home now. It's safer here anyway." He will take me to the apartment I can live at and, you know the best part, he says to me, is that there are other women. This means I don't have to be alone. I can have companionship and all that jazz. In the center of the table we're sitting at are six more fries, and I know he's waiting for me to finish them, so I eat them as slow as possible. I don't want to give him what he's looking for, but I'm also starving.

When he brings me to the apartment that has bags of coke on the entertainment center, there are four other women lying on loveseats in the living room. He doesn't even introduce me by my name because he doesn't know it. I try to decide if it matters as he tells the women to look after me because it's been a while since I've been free. He tells them to take care of me and nods to the bags.

When Jay leaves, the first thing I do is ask the others for their names. I get Tina, which is short for Christina, Louise, which is short for Louisa, Anne, which is actually Margarite's middle name, and Molly, which apparently has nothing to do with her given name. I wait for them to ask for my name, maybe its story or something, but instead Anne stretches herself really long so she can reach one of the bags without having to get up from the sofa. When she wraps her bony fingers around it, she pulls it back against her chest and asks if I'd like to do some with the girls. I try and decide if doing the coke will feel better than them asking for my name, and I decide it will, so I tell her yes. Tina hands me a card to use, to set up my line. I don't know whose it is or where it came from but it doesn't matter. In that moment it is ours. The five of us kneel together, side by side.

I press my nose to the glass table, to the powder, fire, numb. I touch a woman next to me, I don't know who, and I tell her that cocaine increases dopamine and dopamine is in the reward center. I tell her our brains like to reinforce that pleasure. Pleasure. I laugh and touch her neck this time but she doesn't touch me back. She doesn't say anything to me because she's pressed against the glass, her lips curled up, smiling. Smiling. I let her.

I guess I forgot how much I could handle. A little too much after too long without it, or I don't know where it came from and maybe it's laced with something. Too much, too much, and then I swear I feel a moth. My stomach is the moth, and it flutters around inside me. I throw up on the table, on top of the last line we've laid out. I hear a woman say something. Come on, get up. Get up. I don't hear my name. There is no name, so I don't know who she's talking to. I breathe too much before I can't and lay myself back on the carpeted floor, staring at the popcorn ceiling. I feel my skin, wet. My chest is splitting. My heart waves hi to the moth. I hear a woman say something. I think it sounds like Tina. Sounds like Molly. Sounds like me, might be me. I don't know.

The moth bangs. I feel its need to discharge, its desperate attempt to scream that it's there, to escape through my mouth. I think I hear someone ask, What's her name? But no one knows. The moth that makes me nauseous is trying to escape, but I won't let it. Are you sure? Is she okay? I want to tell them my name is Roman, it means strength, but I realize I can't if I'm to keep my mouth shut, and so I force myself to smile a closed-mouth smile as the moth bangs against my insides some more.

EXPECTATIONS

THE MAN TOLD ME ON our first date that the underside of my wrist was beautiful, but when I tell him on our second date that I'm not interested in a relationship with him, my beautiful wrist doesn't matter. He wraps it with his calloused fingers and then wrenches me into him as he says that I shouldn't have led him on. We are in his Ford Pinto, outside the restaurant, because he wanted to leave immediately after I told him the date was going fine, but I'm not interested in anything more going forward. He forgot the greasy pizza leftovers on the table when he said we had to go and left so quickly. In the car he says he's glad he didn't introduce me to his mother who was home when we had to stop there to grab his forgotten wallet. He says he can't believe I kissed him on the first date. He says he really made himself vulnerable with me, and the best I can do is stare out the window as he says all this. A guy rides a bike down the street with a bouquet in his backpack. He looks like he's going somewhere with intention. The guy I'm no longer dating says he'll probably take a break from seeing women again after this, and—Jesus Christ. This guy knows that I'm married. I don't know what he expected.

SOMETHING WORTH IDOLIZING

THE MAGAZINE HAD A PHOTOGRAPH of Lisa Kudrow in a black, crushed velvet dress with long sleeves on the red carpet. You ripped that page out and put the mutilated magazine back on the busted metal rack at the front of the grocery store. You have taped two other photos of celebrities in velvet to your bedroom wall and you can't help but obsess over the idols you see them as.

For weeks you have been dreaming of all the ways you could transform yourself, each new variation pulsing like some sort of heartbeat that keeps you alive, though you're not sure which version you'd choose if you could. But as you stand in the thrift store now, pushing hanger after hanger of tropical button ups, lace tank tops, and vintage nightgowns further away from you on the rack, you can't help but pray for the image that wins to be cheap.

Before you look, you smell her manufactured bubblegum spray. This makes you turn. A woman with a big triangular nose and an entirely pink dress gets too close to you, pushing each hanger even further away from her, almost immediately after you. You say, "Excuse me," even though you have no need to be excused. She just nods. She must be your mother's age, although with her moisturized skin and painted blush, you can't be sure.

When she doesn't move, practically remains a statue, you say, "I'm sorry, I'm still looking at these."

The woman says, "Listen, you have no need to apologize."

You consider telling her what you meant was, Would she step away? You don't.

She has synthetically curled hair. You notice that she's styled the curls so they stay, even though they're thick. If her hair wasn't brown, you might have wished yours looked more like it.

As you stop, she stops, and for a moment you two are caught staring at each other. She has gold, chunky earrings that hang halfway down her neck.

You return to pushing and searching when you finally get to the dresses. They aren't ordered in any special way, not by size, shape, or color, which makes things difficult to find. You are looking for something in particular, after all. Still, each item you touch, the woman touches next.

Maybe ten dresses in, you stop when you find what you're looking for: a velvet dress. It might be floor length depending on the wearer's height, but it's a halter and navy blue. The woman, a knockoff Barbie you've decided, has also stopped, almost in wait.

"That's a little too old for you, hun," she says. Her arms folded at her chest.

The dress you've found is not the same as Lisa's dress, but it's the only reproduction here, so you go pay the three bucks at the register. You do not notice the way it's faded in the center from some old, washed-out stain. You do not know what happened to it in its former life. You do not realize that no one will like it, which is true. No one will like it. You will want to wear it to your first party, but then don't because it's lame. No one will watch you. No one will talk. No one will idolize you.

WE TIME SEX

WE TIME SEX. HOWEVER LONG it takes for him to finish is the time he has to do something I ask for in return. Backrubs, dishes, and taking the dog for a walk are all fair game. We don't even have a dog, but if we did, I'd use sex to get walking it done. I hate walking dogs.

Ollie groans, "Come on, woman. Do we gotta do this again? Can't we just fuck for once?" And I look at his growing braid, his ducktail beard, his faded Levi's fraying at the bottom, and tell him no. We're doing this again. I tell him I want him to clean out the lint trap in the dryer. We don't do that enough around here, and I figure it'll annoy him the most. I remind him that he must stay down there and do this for six minutes this time.

He doesn't say anything and I know it's because he's too busy holding down his hunger. He gets it often, and I see it in his snarl—teeth like little white and yellow tombstones, all rocky and cracked. I know the way those teeth'll bite into me later, but still I will let them. This is because we understand the conditions of our agreement. He takes care of me, but only if I fight his chase, and then once I've been caught, let myself be consumed.

He follows the rules. At exactly six minutes, I hear the rattling of plastic against metal as he slams the trap back into the machine. In no time, he's at the top of the stairs where I am waiting, my arms crossed against my chest as he scoops my body up and carries me just five feet to the hardwood living room floor where he drops me to the ground, me as some sort of caution sign tripped over. He's already unbuttoned his flannel, and I put my hand against his fuzzy chest, telling him just a second. His body over mine, a pause in the moment, I set the timer on my watch.

Okay, go.

Sometimes I think he tries to get it over with as fast as he can so he doesn't have to do chores for any longer than he must. Other times I think that, maybe, he just comes that quick and if he didn't, I might not hate doing this so much.

I would close my eyes, but losing the sense of sight means I feel the pounding more, so I keep them open and stare over his shoulder at the entertainment center.

I think about what he'll have to do next. Maybe it'll be cleaning the toilet. Maybe it'll be pulling weeds. Maybe it'll be drinking some watermelon liquor through a straw with me on the couch watching *The Wonder Years* like we did the first week we met. When he finishes in four and a half minutes, I decide I need him to put the new plate on my buggy. I didn't have one for a while, but almost got pulled over last week after hitting a pothole. The bounce and passing cop car made me cuss out my open window so loud that I thought I might finally need one.

I was standing in the long line to get it, and the guy in front of me wouldn't stop talking about his child's bad report card. I told him that no one cared about the kid's grades. He turned to look at me, and that's when I noticed his sunglasses on inside the Secretary of State building, beneath crummy fluorescent lights that give everyone shadows under their eyes. I couldn't tell if he had those eye shadows or not, on account of the sunglasses hiding them. Maybe the glasses were a smart idea. He said, "Don't worry about me," and then he handed me thirty bucks that smelled like wet wash and told me I should get myself something nice. He said I looked like I needed it. I stared straight at him, chewing on my ring fingernail, when he gave it to me. At least I didn't have to have sex for that exchange.

The man was wearing a brown leather vest like bikers do, with little tassel-y things hanging down from it, and they waved around when he moved. The woman behind me in a housedress and bandana wrapped around her hair told me that the Secretary of State was expensive enough—I should get a personalized license plate. There was a young boy next to her, as tall as her hips, who was chewing gum and blowing bubbles. I asked her why would I waste my money on that, and she told me they mean something. She said hers said D1vaGrl and she spent one whole year setting aside a dollar or two every paycheck to get it. Her sister gave her diamond-looking stickers for her birthday that she stuck to her bumper and now everyone's going to know she ain't cheap.

The rich man ahead of me who was just handing out thirty bucks took his hard-earned place in front of the desk with some employee who had chocolate Scandinavian braids wrapped around her head. He lifted his sunglasses, and I guess she got to see the eyes that I didn't.

I heard the lady behind me say, Michael, then smack the kid in the head—I know this because I heard the smack, it wasn't soft—and then he started whining to her. I was facing forward, not planning on saying anymore to that lady, but then I heard her hush him and start talking again. She said to me that she's going to gift her son her car when it comes time for him to drive. It'll be a while, she said, but when it comes time it'll be his. I turned soon enough to watch the kid spit his gum into his hand and then stick it in the folds of his mom's ankle-length dress. She said, That's all I got. It'll be his legacy.

I told the lady sure, that's nice, and didn't stop thinking about that thirty-dollar personalized plate. I had a lot of time to think about it though, because, well, the Secretary of State's lines take forever. I wished I could have Ollie do that chore instead, but sex with him would never last long enough. After another ten minutes, I decided that the SOS was lucky I was even there getting any kind of plate, let alone something more personalized.

When they finally called my number, I almost missed it. Michael kicked me in the ankle and when I turned around to grab him by his throat, the lady already had him by the hair, pieces of it threaded through her nubby fingers. She said she was so sorry, but it was my turn. She flashed a tacky smile.

The money man passed me, and I smiled at him in a way that I'm actually unfamiliar with, becoming something soft, maybe forgiving. He didn't so much as look at me as I watched his tassels rustle dumbly, and I thought about how he'd probably be the type to make *me* do chores. I wouldn't trade chores for sex though. I'd ask him to give me a nice compliment instead in return.

I thought it was weird that he ignored me, but instead of saying something, I walked up to the next open employee at the counter. As I started to tell the man that I needed a license plate, I smelt leather and campfire which made me stop and scrunch my nose. The man looked at me and smiled. I heard, "How can I help you?" somewhere in front of me, but I was still stuck inside that smell. He smelled exactly like Ollie on the couch with me.

"Ma'am?"

Yeah, I said. I finally told him I needed a license plate and, while he was at it, I wanted it personalized.

He took a form out from under the counter that he gave me to fill out. He accidentally touched my hand without pulling away. I can't be sure, but I think I smiled again for the second time that day.

When the paperwork asked for the personalization, I realized I hadn't thought it through. Getting it was more the principle of the matter since I had never believed I'd have a personalized plate. I wrote down *NO PLATE*. I thought it was funny since I hadn't had one for a while.

The man took one look at the paper before saying I shouldn't go with that choice. Of course I asked why. He told me about some guy who chose that same plate name another time. Everyone thought it was fine. Then he leaned in closer to me, whispered so no one around us could hear our conversation, and he said the man ended up with thousands of dollars in tickets. I guess the problem was when cops wrote tickets and left the license plate space on it blank, the tickets got sent to him.

He told me that wasn't the only time—there were more stories like it, just with other words, like *NULL* and *NO TAG*. He said he'd love to give me a personalized plate, but if I wanted it, to pick another one. I thought it was really nice of him to tell me all that, so I scratched out the *NO PLATE* and wrote in something new.

Here, I told him. Let's do that.

I handed him the clammy cash. The way he thanked me made me think about the chores *this* guy might want me to do, and how if I did them for him, I'd ask him to share a watermelon liquor with me on the couch while watching *The Wonder Years* in return.

As he put the cash in the register, I leaned forward on my elbows, my cleavage clear. He told me to have a nice day.

I walked away from the counter, thinking about the first man who gave me money because "I needed it," and how the second guy gave me advice to save me more. It felt nice to be cared for, but strange—both those men gave me things, but neither wanted anything back.

The woman behind me looked over my shoulder and asked me what my plate meant. Her kid popped a bubble. I let the door's bell jingle behind me on my way out.

I'm lucky this time. It took him six and a half minutes. Which is more than his average. He's going to need the extra time if I want him to put the plate on my car, since that requires unscrewing and screwing and things that take a little while.

He asks me what the job is today, so I tell him. He doesn't groan, which means we both know that the time it takes him to get the tool box from the basement goes toward the time it takes to do the job. I think about how he better move quickly.

He tries to kiss me before he leaves, and I go, *Ah, ah, ah.* I know the rules of this game. It's only if I'm unavailable that he wants me, because men like women they can't have. I must keep this up, because when I make myself available, no one gives a shit.

He gets the box and we're outside. He's holding the plate against my bumper when he says, *FUOG?* He tells me those are weird plate letters. Then he asks me if they stopped putting numbers on plates.

I say, I guess so. I don't tell him it's personalized, or that I thought hard about what I wanted everyone trailing behind me to read.

He says, What a coincidence. My initials are in there.

I go, Huh. Yeah. What a coincidence.

We're silent for another moment. Four minutes into his time and he's only just now getting screws into this new plate, so I'm worried he won't finish early enough.

He starts talking again. He says, It's almost like it's saying, *Fuck you Ollie Gunther.*

Aw, no, baby. I kneel next to him and wrap my arms around his shoulders. I give him a kiss on the cheek. He's still got a minute left, and I never usually interrupt his chore time, but I might have to today.

They really should add some numbers to this, he says. I kiss him on the lips and then pull away.

He rotates the screw driver, but I see him staring at the letters still. I'm deciding if I want him to finish the plate, or if I should do that myself and give him some other chore, but then he makes the decision for me when he picks me up and carries me back to the house.

THESE ARE NOT LOVE LETTERS

I WORK IN A SUPERMARKET AND keep finding odd notes tucked in shelves, under spice jars, behind milk jugs. I find them as I stock, and what do I do with them, I have to do something with them, when they say *what would i do if i killed someone or myself?* I tuck them in my pockets and hold onto them for later because in the unrecognizable handwriting, I recognize something, and that something seems important.

LADYLIKE

ONE BOY WITH A GOLD watch too big for his wrist. Another with a gold chain around his neck that may or may not be fake. The third, much shorter than the others, with sunglasses sitting on his head, tucked in his hair. On top of an overpass.

From the rocky ground below, you watch them wave their arms around at cars driving underneath them, like air dancers outside of cell phone shops. The motion is silly, but also almost welcoming in the way that addressing someone by name is. The tall boy's wristwatch is stuck in his relentless motion and reflects like a mirror when the streetlight hits it just right. The boy flashes the gap between his front teeth when he opens his mouth. He resembles a horse when it neighs.

The other boys continue to wave around him. You notice his blue jeans aren't zipped, and though you aren't surprised, your whole vision splits like light has cut your eyes. *Don't do it.* The boys all laugh—they can't be older than fifteen, and they're acting out of their own troubles, you know, but watching it makes your breath shallow and stilted. You feel angry, but tell yourself that you can choose how you respond. You just want to break something. You try killing the urge to destroy.

Be a lady they say.

You take a tube of sticky cinnamon gloss from your pocket and slather it on your lips. You like the way it burns.

You start walking up the ramp, towards them. They don't seem to notice you, even though you've been watching them for at least ten minutes. You can't help but wonder who waves around for that long, except for asshole teen boys making fools of themselves.

Above you, the summer heat presses against the citrine sky. A jet rips through the inky colors and across the half of the sky that has already turned to night. You notice how far the space between the concrete bridge they stand on and the expressway below them, fast with cars, is. You want to close that distance.

You walk the ramp so you are on the bridge now too. You yell hey to the boys and decide they ignore you. Nothing stops them from waving at passing cars beneath them. You yell hey louder and the horse boy finally turns to look, his eyes all big and black. A boy who hasn't turned yells from the side of his mouth, "Go home!" The horse boy cackles and turns back to the auto-river below him.

The windshield of someone's car reflects the last bit of sun sinking under the horizon. You cover your eyes with both your hands.

When you remove them, you see that the boy with the chain has moved closer to you, and all you can think about is pulling so hard on the necklace that he can't breathe.

"What are you doing?" You ask the boys. You shrink the space between you all as if you are not scared. The wind up here starts pressing your skin, filling your ears. The boy's sunglasses start falling forward, but he catches them before the crash.

"Leave us alone." It's a chorus. All three boys have agreed.

"Fine, if you won't tell me, I'll just wait," and so you sit on the ground, your blue jeans rubbing against the textured concrete, snagging in a spot you don't notice. Your legs crossed as a lady's legs should be.

Horse Boy with the watch groans. One of the others, you aren't sure which, says, "If you're going to stay, you could at least take your shirt off." You realize it's the boy with the glasses, because the one with the chain high-fives him. You consider it for a second, taking your shirt off to reveal your bare skin, then wrapping the fabric across their mouths until they choke.

They glare at you when you blink three times at the light caught in your eye again. The cars swoosh, the wind whelms, and you continue staring, expecting the boys to do something.

"Weird," Horse Boy says, and you notice they've finally stopped waving around.

"Let's just go," the boy with the necklace says. You imagine him still unable to breathe.

"Yeah." The boys don't say goodbye and while barely keeping their pants up around their hips, they march off in the opposite direction from which you came. They must be going home. Might be spending the night together. What a life a boy must have. Do they do the things girls do at sleepovers? Do they tell secrets and share each other's beds?

The day has turned its light off and the citrus twilight is undeniably night now. For a few seconds, you watch the final shapes of their silhouetted figures dissipate into the fresh, endless darkness. No more glints from the boys, but you still want to take all their possessions and destroy them.

The vehicles racing below you are lit by headlights. Splintered colors streaking. They can't see you up above, hidden in shadows. No one knows you're there looking down, watching all of them. You think of the horse boy, his watch, and how it hugged his wrist. You wish he was still next to you, all lank and no muscle, all grin and no bite. You think of smiling soft, at your feet, then at him, then lifting your t-shirt with just your bitty fingers, like you're going to show him what the boy asked for. Then you think of your fingers sliding through his hair, knotting it in your knuckles, and wrenching him to the ground. You dig your heel into his wrist, his watch, the face fractured, pieces of glass buried in the sole of your shoe.

That would give them something to see.

You don't know where anyone below you is going. They're in front of you, then behind you. Swooshing as they pass. Like all the times men drove by before, but you didn't know their destinations. You won't know, never will. They are usually driving a pickup, sometimes a four-door sedan, rarely a van, but they all sound the same. They crack your sense, pull you out. You never ask, just a small slit down your day: a honk. They pull your thoughts, they spill over you, soften against you, a stain, and then they are gone. They always think their honks say something, but all you hear is the spin. All the men make you spin into something they can hold. All you ever hear is the spin, and the honks always stain. You have thought of saying, *Unless you're going to stick around, quit honking at me and leave me alone*, but your voice doesn't sound like a revved engine, so they won't know it. These men are consumed with some kind of ending, but you don't know what it is. You do know, however, that one day the boys watching cars from an overpass will be the men driving the cars below.

You reach into your sweatshirt pockets, which are just big enough to hold the rocks you grabbed from the ground before you walked up here. You think you hear a distant voice saying something about being a lady. You don't have permission to do that. You hear the boys say, Weird, take off your shirt, let's go, and you wish you'd done everything you could to hurt them. You feel stupid for talking yourself out of it. You sense the weight of the rocks, heavy in your pocket, and take them out to cradle them in your palms.

Do it, you say, because the boys won't say it. Or any men. No one's going to give you this permission but you, so you do. You say it and then stand on your tiptoes to reach over the bridge's wire fence and drop the first stone. It falls on the hood of a black Ford Focus, landing like the angel in that most beautiful suicide picture from *LIFE* magazine. The cars swerve as you unload the rest you're holding onto.

There are no boys cat-calling you or men honking, just the symphony of destruction around you. You hear it, luring you in a way those guys never could, and you find this moment rather comforting after all.

FIRST DATE

ONE OF THE MEN I'VE dated has a wooden cross erected in his front yard, and another guy drives a minivan. So as I step away from the high-top table I'm sitting at to use the restroom, my mom who's at the other end of the bar with her third Jack Daniel's stops me to say that this guy who's an actuary and has bought me a drink is a clear step up. She says at least he's got a job and it pays well. It's hard to disagree. She tells me don't fuck it up. He orders another round of drinks while I'm gone and asks the bartender for olives, and then he hands me a martini when I return. I ask how he found this place because it's small and local and no one outside this city knows it. He says he's in town for work, so he pointed his finger to some spot on the map and decided to go there. I guess Bullwinkle's Saloon was the spot. He's in a tailored suit that men from here don't wear, and his short, straw-like hair is combed to the side. He seems like the men in books I've read. Old-man Jim, the only person other than me on the night's lineup, starts playing his guitar on the small bar stage, and then the man in front of me holds out his hand. He asks me if I'd like to dance, and of course I can't say no. I ask him what his name is and he tells me Scott. He says he loved the way I played guitar earlier, the way my delicate fingers pulled the strings with intention in front of an audience. He says he could tell I know how to perform. He asks me how long I've been playing as he spins me in a circle and I can't help but think, nearly my whole life. I tell him, for an audience, maybe five years. He seems satisfied. Scott asks what other talents I have and I tell him that I also read palms. He asks if I could read his and I say yes, even if I am uncertain. He doesn't remove it from my hand as he guides me around our table, but without even looking at it, I know this: I could tell him one thing, or another, and my reading would be just as successful either way. I should tell him that I'm actually more interested in the things that convince us something is true even if it isn't. But I don't. My mom, on what looks like her fourth drink now, winks at me from across the room. She nods her head.

ANATOMY OF DESIRE

I THOUGHT LOVE WOULD TASTE different than a cigarette (but it didn't). That's what Scott tastes like anyway, and he's the one I married. The one I love. But I find it so hard to love intimately when he spends days in airplanes, days in corporate offices with too much natural light because of the big glass windows that skyscrapers are built with. He kisses me like I'm something bitter, polite but undesirable, when he's the one who tastes tart. I didn't ask him to marry me. He asked me. And when I went into a Barnes & Noble and saw a man in the first aisle I walked down, thumbing through chocolate-making books, I had to stop him with just my hand, the same hand that held Scott's when he placed a wedding band on my finger, and ask if he made chocolate frequently. I had to admit to him that I make chocolate myself, on locked nights that are cold, and watch it drizzle down when I lift the spoon. He told me he did, about how he ate most of it on his own. And when I smiled at the man in the canned food aisle at the grocery store, he smiled back, and we spoke of eating off people's plates, taking what we like best, or don't like and eating it anyway, the whole way to the register, and even though I'm married, he gave me his number. It wasn't in a sly or inappropriate way, but some kind of genuine way that I understood. And when I ended up drunk at my friend's wedding that Scott had to miss, was working in Austin that weekend, I felt the let and go that one feels when pulled into someone whose hand on their spine guides them like a marionette on the dance floor. My arms were caught between us, pressed against my chest, his chest, our lips almost touching during the slow song after some spins during the fast songs. And I know it's wrong to say it, even wronger to think it to begin with, but I think of these men often. Some I still talk to, smile when they text me about an inside joke we've shared over the last year. Have never cheated, never kissed them, but in another world, I think of their husky breath left on my shoulders, their fingers pressed into my flesh, an eyelash left on my cheek. I think of what it might be like to be romanced with a good morning message, and even though I am happy my husband is here, grateful for his support, I think about his death. About how if he dies, what it would be like to cling to another man's sweat-dewed body in a way that feels impatient and necessary.

LOCATE THE HEART LINE

I THINK, *SHE'S DOING IT* wrong. *How does she look so good?* seconds into entering my room for something I no longer remember, and finding my husband Scott fucking a nymph in our bed, his thick waist overpowering her soft belly and most of her hidden beneath his weight. I notice her wrists are tied too tight against the headboard. I'm not sure where the ropes came from, but I know they are too constricting. She must not know that hands above the head can increase the risk of fainting. About a minute into standing in my bedroom doorway—a doorway that faces my side of the bed—and my conniving husband pressing his fat fingers into whatever spaces he can find on her body, I start to read the palm of hers that faces me. There is a long life line; it's easy to see. That means she is vibrant. The money line is also obvious. It emerges from the life line which shows that she is ambitious. And because it is long and clear, running from her wrist to her middle finger, she has a lucky future. The last thing I notice is that her fire-shaped hand shows she's stimulated by a desire to do things boldly. I guess that is why her fleshy legs are opened wide and spread across my side. Scott moves his hand to her lips, sticks his thumb in, down her throat maybe, then covers her whole mouth completely with his big hand. I cannot see his palm. Scott's siren moans, but he muffles her sound. From his side I watch him smile. It has been a long time since I have known him to be happy like he is in this moment. I guess she could be everything he wants. Then with a voluminous moan, she looks over Scott's shoulder and accidentally straight at me. I do not wipe the understated rage from my face. As Scott notices the sudden look of surprise on hers, he turns back to see me too, and I leave him there like that. Walking to the front door, I pick up her shoes. They are little black ballet flats that do not look like something this harlequin would wear, and I'm still not sure how I missed them when I first got home. I walked right past them. Now I pick the shoes up, put them in the freezer, and walk out the front door, locking it behind me. It was a little hard to tell from where I was standing in the doorway, but from what I saw, I think her heart line was short and straight. That means that she has little interest in expressing love or romance. Maybe the little charmer is perfect for him after all.

YOUNG AND RECKLESS

JASON, THE SCHOOL'S QUARTERBACK, WAS huddled in the corner behind the basement's pool table with a group of six kids surrounding him and a condom halfway up his nose. The overhead fluorescents were off, but a few applique gold floor lamps that buzzed like insects cast weird streams of light around the space.

I heard Stan tell Jason to hurry up, and then Stan mocked him: isn't this like your tenth time doing it or something?

And it was true. Jason was known for excelling at the condom snorting challenge. A challenge that only a few took on because it requires exactly what it sounds like: sticking one of those rubbers in your nostril, breathing in as hard as you can, sliding it through your throat, and pulling it out of your mouth.

But there Jason was, might've actually been his fifteenth time doing it, wrinkled up with pain and embarrassment, unable to snort the latex down his pharynx this time. He gagged, his skin furrowed like the folds on a Shar Pei, and the crowd booed.

Jason. Get it together.

I watched spit drip out of his mouth as he second-guessed the whole thing and almost began to pull the penis-straitjacket back out his nose. The crowd booed louder. Don't forget though—he was a quarterback, not a quitter. Also, the condom got stuck.

For a split second, Jason had to consider what might've been the hardest decision of his life: pull it harder out his nose and dislodge, or reach back in his mouth and hope he could slide it out the way he originally planned.

The girl that Jason thought he liked watched him as he cried. Our idiot spent eleven seconds unable to breathe because of this escapade, and then he finally got it out through his mouth, the way he'd planned all along.

The kids around him cheered, myself included, and some patted him on his back, as he cried out, "Oh my God," swallowing the biggest gulp of air in his life.

What's funny about this story isn't that Jason made a fool of himself, but rather that this was all going on right behind Loose Leslie sitting on the couch, because unlike Jason, she didn't use condoms.

Leslie was seventeen, I mean, a lot of us were. While the party in the basement had been booing (and then cheering) Jason, she was rubbing her wet fingers along the couch's burgundy velvet, dragging temporary lines in the fabric. She held a red Solo cup in her right hand with her name in Sharpie, all caps, on the front. Some of the sloppy drink dripped down the side, leaving her fingers wet and sticky. She was two drinks in and, yeah, we were young, but most of us knew that alcohol and babies didn't mix, and she was clearly pregnant. I think that's why Stan, with his wrestling shoulders and black ponytail, sat right on top of the velvet portraits she was drawing after the condom commotion died. He had to have known her guard was down.

Then at the worst time he could, Leslie's boyfriend Drew clunked down the stairs in his chunky sneakers when he caught her pressed against Stan, her fingers slipped between his locks, and her beer breath stuck to his neck. Drew wasted no time flipping the mid-century coffee table in front of the couch so that one of its wooden legs came loose. He told her to fuck off.

Mitch said, "Ha ha, that's incredible," when we almost got hit but missed from where we stood. I rolled my eyes, but I didn't think Mitch saw, and I told him I'd be back, even though I wouldn't be. See, I had desperately wanted attention that night, and he really wanted to show someone his new scar leftover from some stitches on his knee. He fell playing lacrosse or something. But he blushed when I lied and told him the scar was cool (how lame), and then he wouldn't talk about anything else, so I was no longer interested.

As I walked away from Mitch, Drew, who was right there, put his hand against the small of my back. "Do you want to be here? Let's go somewhere else," he said, motioning toward the stairs.

First Leslie got pregnant. Then after that night, all of Richard M. Ross High School thought I slept with her ex-boyfriend. Well, everyone except Leslie.

But I didn't do that—sleep with Drew—and I'm sure I'm not the reason he broke up with her. There were a million things the girl could have done to make him break up with her.

But I was over the party. I had gotten nowhere with Mitch, and wasn't particularly interested in anyone from the condom crew.

So when Drew pushed me on no accord of my own, I let him. We wove through the throng of kids swaying, smushed against each other, sitting on countertops in the kitchen, then out the back door, and I left the unfinished drink I had on a table because that High Life was the cheapest alcohol at any of the parties I'd been to.

The house was down the street from a park. That's when me and Drew, two kinda-drunk high schoolers, lay down on a merry-go-round, staring up at the smashed-glass of stars.

"What a bitch," Drew said as he bent his arms across his chest. "She did a lot of shady things, you know."

"Yeah, I heard."

"I don't even know if that baby's mine, I guess."

I wondered what it would be like to not know if a kid was yours. I didn't have that luxury.

A breeze blew past us and Drew pulled his hood up over his head. He said, "You know, some people have an irrational fear of what others think."

"Sure." I couldn't tell if that was meant to be a question or a comment.

He added quickly, "No idea why."

I thought about how some people have been told what to be like for so long that who they are disappears. They don't even know how to think of themselves outside of the expectations that are shoved down their throats. It's those people who care a lot about what others think, and I was one of those people.

My ex was a football player who asked me if I'd meet him at the mall for our first date. I spent all morning putting on eyeliner and mascara and layering different shirts so that by the time I was finished I was embarrassingly sweaty. When we sat in the food court though, he told me that I had nice lips, and that he'd never known anyone like me. He knew how to make butterflies happen, and I fell in love immediately. He asked me to be his girlfriend after school the next week at the bus stop, and of course I said yes.

Then not even two months later, we were leaving the movie theater when he told me he had something he needed to say. I said sure, go ahead and say it, but I could have never guessed what would come out of his mouth next. He said I was pretty, but if I lost some weight, I'd be hotter. I don't remember how I responded, but I remember feeling like I died. He swore he wasn't being mean, and that he was just looking out for me. He wanted me to be the best version of myself I could be, and when I looked in the mirror later, I agreed with him. Of course he was right.

Drew added to his thought on irrational fears. "There's even a name for that phenomenon, which I think is weird," although he never did give it.

I knew Drew from English class where we had to write a poem, and he read his aloud. It could have been about anything we wanted, but he wrote about Leslie. I knew it was about her because he mentioned her dirty, straw-colored hair, and the freckle on her pointer finger, except he talked about those two things nicer in it. He also described the slender, hourglass figure she had, and I guess even if she annoyed me, I felt a little in love with her too by the time he finished reading.

Drew said, "The pizza in the cafeteria last week sucked."

"Sure did."

He used his feet to push the metal merry-go-round slab that we were spread across in a circle. Some stones below the structure made clacking noises. The stars moved slightly, and it looked like someone had kicked the glass pile apart. I rolled into his side and pressed against his warm body, hoping he didn't notice my shape. He talked some more about school lunches, and even though I didn't give a shit, I listened and nodded and then left my head against his shoulder when I finished.

I felt bad for Drew.

It wasn't his fault Leslie got around, got pregnant, and got drunk. She was young and reckless. So he had to know there was no way things would end well if she stayed on that path. I'd heard about all kinds of things that have happened to women who, like Leslie, made bad decisions. On the morning news, for example, the lady anchor with chunky gold earrings said two men lit a pregnant woman on fire. The next month, the same station reported that a school shooter's mom drank heavily when she was pregnant, so who's to say that didn't influence his choices? Then my cousin told us over Thanksgiving dinner that a woman she knew had given birth to a girl with Fetal Alcohol Syndrome, and now the twenty-six-year-old acts like a first grader.

It was hard for me to hate Leslie completely though, because babies make you ugly. They make you undesirable. The stomach fat, wide hips, stretch marks, swollen feet and toes, loose vagina, and boobs that resemble deflated balloons. You become a person people don't like to look at. A person they'd never actually want to be or be with. Who wants to live like that? Then, to make it all worse, on top of an oversized, warped body and getting lit on fire, I mean, you're pregnant, so you end up with a kid—and you're supposed to keep that kid alive.

I don't like to admit this, but I know all of this is true because I'd been pregnant once too.

I spent the next few months with my nose in magazines, reading about movie stars and how they attracted men. About what they ate. So I dieted. I looked at how they dressed. I imitated their makeup. I did everything I could to reincarnate myself. That's why, when I sat in the big handicap stall in the supermarket bathroom (so I could comfortably spread my legs over the toilet and piss on a stick) and realized two lines had showed up on the test I swiped, I wanted it gone.

I never told Ethan what I did. Sex had finally started improving because he remembered lube, he agreed to do it in someplace other than a car, and he finally stopped talking (he said those rude things when he talked). I had also lost two pounds and was working on losing some more. I didn't want to ruin things.

Keeping the secret didn't matter though. He broke up with me just nine months into our relationship anyway, and on the one-month anniversary of my abortion too.

So while I didn't know what else to say except *Leslie was bad*—bad and pregnant—I empathized a little.

Drew started sitting next to me in class. He'd write me small notes that he'd fold up and pass to me when our teacher turned around. One said lunch the day before sucked. I gave him a thumbs up. Another said our teacher was a prick and I made sure to throw that one out. After a week of this, he passed me one that said he was going to the football game. I wrote cool and passed it back. He asked if I was going and even though I wasn't planning on it, I told him yes, and he wrote back that he'd see me there.

Then squished in the bleachers by superfan parents yelling at the coaches, my gangly knees crushed together, Drew got shoved into me but didn't try too hard to move away. His hand slid onto mine. His mouth against my ear, he half-shouted so I could hear that we should get some food after. I nodded my head yes.

Sitting in the twenty-four-hour McDonald's parking lot with a large fry and two strawberry shakes, he told me I had something on my mouth, he could get it off, and then he kissed me. Then he asked if I knew Leslie well but, like, what? I didn't care. I told him no, because I didn't. He sighed and told me it's easy to love and hate her. He wasn't sure which one he was feeling half the time. I kissed him back, but had the thought of Leslie kissing him with her sloppy-seconds lips at the same time. I wondered if he liked that she was pregnant. He kissed me again and then reached for a few fries.

Leslie and I didn't have any classes together. We didn't even have the same lunch. If I'm being honest, I only ever saw her up close in person at the party, so I had to go out of my way to find her at school. She was next to the vending machine, rummaging through her purse for another quarter. She mumbled something about wanting some hot chips. She was even bigger than she was the night Jason almost died snorting condoms.

So I did what I had to do and took a quarter out of the change purse I carried with me. Put it on the security desk next to the machine, set it down in a way that it made a loud noise so she'd notice, and just tipped my head down at the coin when she looked at it. Like, here you go. That asshole took the quarter, shoved it hard into the machine, and pressed the button that dropped some regular potato chips down. She didn't even say thank you.

She ripped the flimsy chip bag open with her teeth and walked away.

"Hey," I called after her, skipping a little to catch up.

"What?" She put one potato chip between her teeth and crunched.

I looked at the way her fitted tank top didn't actually fit her and instead naturally rolled up, revealing her big belly and red tiger stripes. I thought about how Leslie could be a mother soon. Too soon.

I asked her how everything was going, all things considered. She shrugged, her shoulders like little whack-a-moles, popping up.

I pointed at her bowling-ball-belly and asked how the kid was.

"Big," she said.

She put another few chips between her teeth. By this time, she was wearing slippers to school and shuffled along the hallways lined with aluminum foil gum wrappers, loose hair, and dust. These scraps would get caught on the fuzzy fabric of her shoes.

After some thought, and me following her wobbles to whatever class she was going to that I didn't have, she added, "Bigger than I asked for."

I wasn't sure what she expected after getting pregnant, but pregnant bitches get bigger. Like, a lot bigger.

"Did you want this?"

After a pause, "No."

She wasn't breathing much, kind of wheezing, and carrying some books in her bent elbow. The one on top was titled *Disturbance: An American History*. I wondered if she'd been lying to all of us and was further along than she said.

She added, "My momma doesn't even care."

"Oh?"

"Yeah." She sat down in a blue, plastic chair in the hallway outside a classroom. The legs on it squeaked. It wasn't for her, but she made it hers. I considered telling her that we should probably move on, the bell rang a few minutes ago and all, but I didn't.

"She had me when she was fifteen. When did your momma have you?"

I wasn't sure. Maybe twenty-five? I told Leslie, "Close to thirty."

"Huh. So she had it all figured out when she had you."

I couldn't have been sure at that time, but I said to her, "I don't think anyone ever has it figured out." I do think what I said is true. I'm pretty sure my mom knew as little about raising me as Leslie's mom did.

"That's scary."

"Yeah, I guess so. You actually afraid of that?" I looked at the exercise-ball fixture she had.

She nodded her head. Then seemingly changing subjects, she said, "You know, I've been craving hot chips and root beer floats."

I had never gotten far enough along in my pregnancy to get cravings, but root beer floats were actually my favorite dessert, so I had to admit she had good taste.

"How far along are you?"

"A little over five months, I think." She looked a lot bigger.

"Has anyone talked to you about your other options?" I asked.

Mrs. Farley walked past us in the hallway, stopped to do a double-take, and asked us where we were supposed to be. The rhinestone chain hanging from her cat-eye glasses shook and shimmered when she came to a halt.

Leslie said she was having pregnancy pains and that our teacher told us we could come out here for a minute to cool off and, like, that's all it took. Unsure of what to say, worried it might be against the law probably, Mrs. Farley just walked away.

Leslie said, "What options?"

I told her she could have her life back, and she wouldn't have to get bigger. I mean, she wouldn't have to wobble around like this. If she really was five months along, she may be right at that cusp.

"I miss Drew. It can't be anyone's but his." She ignored what I had said.

I didn't believe that, the second part I mean, but I believed she missed Drew. I wasn't sure what kind of shot she had with him at that point though. He was calling me a few times a week.

She asked if I'd walk up to the liquor store and get some hot chips after school with her and I agreed to.

On the way there, I learned all about how she had a thing for roller coasters and rainbow parties too. She knew some guys that worked at the amusement park an hour away, and they'd let her on rides even when the signs said no pregnant women. All it took was pulling a few tubes of lipstick out of her purse and letting the guy lead her to a staff bathroom. With an unconcerned swoop, she'd rub a color on her lip and drop to her knees.

"Take down your pants," she'd say, "or would you like me to do it for you?" Whatever the guy wanted was okay. She'd even ask which color he'd like her to start with.

By the time she finished running her lips down him as many times as the number of colors she had, the boy had a rainbow and a reason to let her ride some rides.

Pregnant ladies are not allowed on things like roller coasters and the Ring of Fire because they flip you upside down, back and forth, and shake you like fresh popcorn. Things move when you shake like that, and the placenta detaches from the womb. Then the baby gets deprived of things it needs like oxygen and nutrients, and this is why spinning at tens of miles an hour is bad. But Leslie would put on her shorts and crop top that summer, sunglasses to protect those retinas, and find a way to get to the park at least three times, and she was proud of it. She called herself resourceful. She must've wanted her baby breathing like Jason with a condom in his nose. That poor kid.

The thing is, some girls just aren't fit to be mothers, and since Leslie's poor choices didn't stop at drinking, it was clear she needed help with more than her looks.

Sitting on one of those concrete parking stops outside the liquor store, Leslie dug her hand into her hot chips bag and I told her more about the clinic. I told her that her life was going to change with this baby, and then I asked if she wanted that. She nodded her head and licked her fingers and then dried them off on the ends of her rolled up shirt. She said, "How much?" Like she didn't know how this parasite eating all the hot chips she just swallowed was going to transform her life. Like, did she not understand what she was carrying around?

I just looked at her and said, "A lot."

I could see her thinking about it. Maybe she was trying to decide if that was good or bad, but I didn't see anything good about it.

"It might not be so bad. I told you my momma had me when she was young."

"Is your mom happy?"

"I think so." She grabbed some more hot chips from the bag. She crunched the chips, red powder smeared all over her teeth, and she added, "She loves all us kids anyway."

"You have siblings?"

"Yeah. Five."

Leslie tried to get up but couldn't find her balance and almost fell face down into the busted parking lot. I stood up to reach my hand out and help her, instantly regretting it when her red and orange, spitty hands gripped mine.

"That's a big family," I told her.

"Not really. I only live with one. The other four live with their daddies."

When she finally caught her balance, I wiped my hands off on my pants and said, "Do you know your dad?"

She kinda cackled and said no.

"Do you like that?"

She shrugged and said, "It'd be nice to know my daddy, but sometimes you can't."

We started walking back toward the school and passed the bus stop where Ethan first asked me to be his girlfriend.

I asked Leslie, "Is that what you want for your baby?"

She didn't say anything for a minute. Then she finally said, "No, but it doesn't matter what I want."

"Listen, Leslie. Yes it does." I tried convincing her that she had a lot to lose, but I was failing, and I hated that. The more I learned about her, the more I rooted for her.

"It literally doesn't. What I want gets me in trouble, and even if I don't want it, what I do gets me in trouble. Like I don't *want* to flirt with everyone, but I *do*. And I get hurt. I didn't want to upset Drew, but I did. I screwed it up, so now it's just me and this little nugget," she said, looking down. "Maybe this will help me change."

I looked down at myself too, wondering if the no-calorie Cokes and sugar-free substitutes I'd been using were helping my own figure at all.

"What I'm saying is you don't have to do this alone."

"Raise a kid?"

"Or have it. You don't have to ruin your life."

"Look, I shouldn't have said anything. I'm fine. Let's just keep this between us."

We had about a block left to school, and I felt worse than before for Leslie, even if she did do it all to herself.

"But it's not fair to you. I can make the call with you if you want. Just see how the doctors can help you, maybe."

I dug around in my pocket for some change, ready to lend Leslie some more if she decided to use the payphone.

Leslie found me during passing time the next day to ask if I thought she could be better. "A better person that is."

I looked at her from the side of my eyes and asked, "What's that supposed to mean?"

She hobbled along, pushing her way through the crowded hallway. "I want to be a better person, like someone people respect, and what you said yesterday got me thinking." She sighed a big sigh. "Maybe a baby won't make me better."

I could tell she felt helpless by the way her shoulders sagged. Patrick, who walked past us in the opposite direction, looked at me kinda funny, but he didn't understand, so I put my arm around Leslie's shoulders and reminded her that she had options, like, she could have some control. Then I said, if she wanted, I'd still help her make the call.

I had to look the number up in a phone book after school, but making the appointment was easy enough after that.

On the day of her consultation, Leslie sat in my passenger seat with her hands folded on her lap. She had on a peasant skirt and crop top, and while none of it matched, it didn't seem to bother her. She said, "I guess I'm doing this."

We pulled up to the building and a group of five people stood out front. They had signs duct taped to wooden poles that said things like SAVE THE BABIES and YOURE GOING TO HELL. One sign had a zoomed in, blurry photograph of a bunch of bloody bits and pieces that they painted the words THIS COULD BE UR BABY over.

"Whatever you do, don't listen to them," I said. "Just look straight ahead." I knew the kind of fear their imaginary horror stories could put in a girl, and it would derail her whole future.

Leslie nodded, but the minute we got out of the car and started walking, the old man in the group, the one with the sign that said YOURE GOING TO HELL started yelling to Leslie that the devil was inside her and she was promised a trip to Hell for murdering her baby. The old woman with a rosary wrapped around her wrist added that, yeah, she should love her baby like Jesus loves her.

Leslie didn't take my advice. Instead, she turned to the group and started cussing up a storm. She told them to fuck off, they didn't know her, and why don't they go to Hell if they know so much about it.

I tried to say, Shhh, Leslie, and grabbed on her arm to pull her along, but she couldn't stop herself.

The crowd booed her and she barked at them and I pulled down my dress a little and finally I got Leslie inside the front door, which I made sure shut tight behind us.

She said, "Wow. What a riot," then didn't even want to go up to the desk and sign in.

"You have to," I said to her. "This is your only shot." That bun sitting in her oven was too far along to wait any longer. Even a day more and they'd maybe have to tell her she couldn't do it, and we couldn't have that. I nudged her again to go up to the desk. Girls have to stick together.

The woman behind the glass window had on a name tag that said Sherri, and it had two holographic flower stickers on it. Her nails were painted hot pink and she had a large wad of bubble gum in her mouth. It was easy to recognize her, even though I don't think she recognized me. She had been working the day I went there too.

"How far along are you?" She asked, and Leslie told her the same thing she told me. Five months. The woman looked doubtful. "I'm going to be honest. We might not be able to do anything for you, sweetheart, but the doctor will let you know. Go on and sit down. It might take a while, and your friend will have to wait when you go back."

"Sure," Leslie said.

We sat down in some bony chairs and listened to the oldies on the overhead radio. During that time, Leslie said, "Do you think if I do this, Drew can love me?"

I didn't tell her that I picked Drew up last week, and we parked behind the mall where kids go to make out. By then, I no longer thought about if he cared that she was pregnant or not. I mean, he didn't have to care, after all. If the baby actually was his, it didn't make a difference. Boys could get away scot-free with their mistakes.

I told her maybe.

She scrunched her face, but I couldn't tell if it was because of what I said or the song that started on the radio. She let out a heavy sigh and stood up to leave.

I told her to stop. To think about it. Was she ready for a child? This was her last chance. She shook her head. For one last try, I reminded her that she didn't have to look like this, but that didn't seem to bother her like it did me.

On her way out the door, me following behind, I noticed three new people standing on the sidewalk. One had a sign that said, LOVE IS THE ANSWER, and then Leslie went right ahead and showed those people the most love she could in that moment. She didn't say anything.

Leslie had me drop her off at her place, and I saw one of her little sisters running around the front lawn without a shirt on. For the first time, Leslie thanked me, then hobbled her way inside the house with her sister chasing after her.

I couldn't believe that she'd given up. We were so close.

I just hoped she was right and that the baby might help her grow up a little.

We found out Leslie killed herself the next week over an announcement our principal Mr. Harrison gave during sixth hour. There was a moment of silence for her and the baby.

en though he could be lying about liking me and
never know, and I can't miss my shot.
e I was going to the movies with a group of
e was going to join. I almost died. My mom said
m another girl's mom that he was bad news, and
d flimsy joints and almost got caught with them
he asked me if he smoked pot, and I told her
ugh I shouldn't have, so she kept going on and
f he starts smoking, to call her, and I told her I
I won't, because I'd never leave Nick at a party
herever else alone with my mom picking me
paranoid he's a drug addict or something. She
a turn her baby girl into a loser.
ng enough to run my fingers through, which
rs a little too much makeup around his eyes
ctually complements their blue color nicely
nything about it to anyone.
at my acquaintance-friend Chris's house,
ment, and mostly just like twelve people,
with, but a lot I don't even know, and a
re trying to turn Go Fish into a drinking
ere has to be better parties than this, but
n't complain too much. There's a saggy,
ur other people too that I'm sitting on
of the others to pass me whatever it is
nk enough so I don't really have to talk
meone says something that's supposed
ch them all drink every time someone

Jason broke the silence and said that's what she gets for drinking when pregnant—everybody knows how bad that is.

Rumors spread quickly that she swallowed a bunch of drugs her mom had stored in the bathroom. I also heard she shot herself when no one was home, although I don't know where she'd have gotten the gun. I don't know the best way to go, but I hoped however it happened it was quick.

We never found out the truth, but wow. Leslie was gone, and while it's true we all thought she was a trainwreck, a kind of crash you couldn't take your eyes off, some part of me knew that she and I weren't too different.

I saw Drew on my way out of school. He stopped me near the front doors and told me he'd walk me to my car. I shrugged and let him, although I knew what it meant. Five minutes later we were inside the vehicle, windows down, in the half-empty parking lot with some kids walking past to their own beater cars. He leaned in to kiss me, and I let him, even though his breath felt heavy in a way that seemed inappropriate for three in the afternoon on a school day. It was weird, too, because after he brought up Leslie most of the times we made out for the last month, he didn't say anything about her then. It's like she no longer existed, and maybe she didn't, but ignoring her felt wrong. The other thing about Leslie dying is that she wasn't the only one. Drew didn't say anything about the baby either.

Our bodies were crammed in the sweaty seats, knocking into roadblocks like the wheel and center cup holders we were used to, and I thought about Ethan. I couldn't help it. I was curious about where he was and what he was thinking of during Mr. Harrison's announcement. Did it surprise him? Did it upset him? Did he know Leslie? He had to have. We all did. Did he even listen to the announcement? I wondered how he might have felt last year if I had died too instead of just his baby he never knew of.

I drove Drew home and didn't wait to see his family. He didn't thank me. He only said he'd see me the next day, and then he shut the door. I didn't wait for him to walk inside before I left.

Would you believe me if I told you that on the day Leslie died, I finally realized what I'd been missing all along? No one spoke it to me, but they didn't have to. It came to me in the silence.

It didn't matter what you did or who you tried to please. I mean, you could recreate yourself as many times as you wanted, but you'd still fall short. Everyone expects girls to follow the rules and be perfect all the time, but then won't say what happens when the girls no longer can.

I stopped at the corner drugstore before going home. I walked down the makeup aisle and grabbed a few things. When I went to check out, the young woman just a few years older than me who was working the register rolled my mascara in her hand before ringing it up. She said, "I've been eyeing this brand for a while. Does it work?"

And I thought, a girl who's trying to please people has everything to lose, so a girl can't win after all.

has to pull a card, I think. I don't know. I stop paying attention to the rules and just drink when everyone else drinks.

From my seat, I watch Nick nurse a bag of cold vegetables. I guess he hurt something. Then Veronica and Leanne, who are sitting on the loveseat across from me, must suddenly feel important enough because of the alcohol I suppose, to say they see me watching Nick. I don't yet feel important enough, but I tell them to shut up anyway. They laugh and call out to him, and now everyone's watching him hold a bag of frozen corn to his arm while he talks to a little skinny girl and makes a dumb face. He ignores Veronica and Leanne, hands his girl the bag and goes to the other side of the basement where there is a sailor hat hanging on the wall next to some certificate that's for a person who died in the Navy. He takes the hat though.

Nick hasn't said hi to me tonight even though he was here before I was, and I've been here for at least an hour. Maybe it's because he's nervous. Boys can feel that too, sometimes. I drink some more of whatever that other guy gave me and accidentally miss my mouth so some drips onto my jeans.

Then Nick goes back over to the little twiggy girl with ratty hair and two belts around her waist, and puts his hands out and rotates them in a circle like he's driving a boat. She doesn't exactly laugh, but he does, and he leans in to kiss her but pulls the old hat down so it hides their faces. They are leaning against the washing machine.

I have someone's legs on my lap that I push off immediately, and I walk over to them two kissers very quickly and say, Nick, and ask him what's going on. It's finally time to address the elephant in the room. So he takes down the sailor's hat and looks at me like he's got no clue, and I bet he has no clue, because he's a boy, and they just don't get it sometimes. I say it again, Why? What's going on? And I hear a whole roomful of laughs behind me, and over on the side of me, and Victoria yells, *Loser*, and more laughs and she adds, He's just not into you, and Nick winks at her.

Nick had a date to Homecoming say *no* last minute one time but went to the dance anyway with a group of us, and he didn't dance with me, but I just thought it was because he liked me and was too embarrassed to ask. Then there was a different time that his friend dropped him and the chemistry book I lent him off at my front door, with his friend illegally parked across the street. And then he left me that voicemail, and even though he never talks to me in public, except when another girl's around and he flirts with me, I love him so much and he said he loved me too in that voicemail, so I take the hat right outta his hands and I throw it on the floor next to our bare feet, and even though the skinny girl is still standing so close I can feel her arm touch mine, I lift my hands up to his cheeks and I pull him in and kiss him so hard it's not even sexy or enjoyable. The laughter is soft compared to the blood rushing in my eardrums and I feel Nick pulling away so hard, which must mean that he's playing hard to get, like he wants me to prove I want him, so I grip his flesh tighter, like I'm trying to hold onto this moment forever. Finally we part for air and I hear a whistle and some stomps and laughs and Nick shakes his head and wipes my saliva off his mouth and tells me I'm a fucking idiot. The girl he kissed before me is gone, I don't know where she went, but a girl named Sam who I also saw him kiss at the café one time calls out from behind me, "He's not into you, loser."

I know Sam from elementary school when I spent the night at her cousin's house and we played truth or dare. She dared me to flash everyone, so I lifted my stained princess pajamas and showed the small buds of my nipples. This is the first time she's talked to me since.

I turn to the audience now wrapped around me, and I smile, my mouth swollen with adrenaline from touching him.

Someone says *oww oww* like a siren and I think of the time he brought me that chemistry book and how a cop car pulled up. Nick grabbed me by my shoulders and pushed me in front of him like a shield. Cop lights were spinning, a siren was screaming, but the cop drove past us and then Dave Emmerson pulled up and Nick said Dave's lucky because he had weed in his car and couldn't get caught like that. It was an uncomfortably cold evening, my feet pressed against the concrete porch, and Nick in a t-shirt. I wanted more than anything to kiss him there, but he said See ya later and got in Dave's car and left.

I realize Sam is making kissy faces, and Veronica is making them back, and Nick has walked away. I smile a big trophy smile at him, but he doesn't see it because he's shaking his head no and saying, "Gross." He's saying, "Loser." I'm holding my smile because if I don't that might mean I have lost, and for a minute it felt like I won, but now I can't breathe and I don't know if it's blood or breath that's draining from me. Some of his eye makeup's left on my forehead where I pulled him in, the feel of his soft boy skin still in my hands, the smell of his shirt I don't think he's washed, stunned that this really happened, astonished that he said he didn't want it. Because how could he not feel it, how could he not want it too, I thought all signs pointed to yes, we have to be soulmates, right? But I guess a boy pulling away isn't playing hard to get, after all.

I'll play the other game then. Hard to win. I'm gonna play hard to win because I know there's a bunch of people behind me, lined up like an opposing team's fans, waiting for me to lose, but that's not how this is going to end. No. My mom didn't raise a loser.

TARNISHED

WE HAD ELOPED ON THE Oregon Coast, where neither of us had been before, and then drove round and round up the mountains to some stranger's cabin we rented for the night. The lush trees towered over us, and the moonlight-glazed water crashed down below. I had to tell my husband to stop driving before I opened the passenger door, stuck my head out, and threw up on the ground of the mountain there. Got a little on my white dress. He won't let me live it down, and to this day he still brings up the time I threw up on our wedding night before I even drank.

My husband is down the hall, singing in the shower, and I am tucked in our bed underneath sheets he hasn't washed. A cheap, tarnished ring with a pastel heart gem is on his nightstand. I know it belongs to a girly woman. I could bring up the way it is made of materials that are such low quality and will most likely get forgotten. I could remind him of the pearl necklace I found, most likely fake, left in the couch cushions two years ago. The clasp was broken, and whatever woman it belonged to didn't get that one back either. I *could* choose to not let him live it down. But I won't. I will not ask him about it. He will not mention it. We will get into bed, and when he leans in to kiss me good night, I will not tell him that he fucked up our marriage without even knowing.

SHEDDING

THE THING IS, HEATHER'S HAIR is beautiful. It's a Midnight Blue Black color, long, thick, and usually done in some sort of fancy style. One day it's a classic beehive and the next it's Hollywood curls. You've seen her wear it down before too, so you know that there are layers in it that give it the extra volume that you wished you had, but she could also cut it all off and go short if she wanted, and it would still look good. You love Heather's hair.

You met Heather when you found her ad for a roommate in the newspaper. She answered your phone call, invited you to see the place—a one-bedroom apartment—and that was when you first fell in love. You've dreamt of having hair like hers your whole life.

She gave you a very brief tour (during which you mostly looked at the back of her head). The two twin-sized beds in the little room were cramped, but that made it cheaper, and it's really all you could afford for the first time out of your mother's. It wasn't until after you moved in that you realized you hadn't seen the inside of the shower during your brief tour, because why would you?

Some women shed in the shower. Heather does. Then she pulls all the strands of hair off her body and sticks them against the wet shower wall where she leaves them. You find new strands every time you get in.

Standing there now, you try to enjoy the scalding water that's searing your skin the way women like it, but Heather's wet strands are twisted in front of you. They looked like a snake earlier this week, but because now there's more, and because Heather's hair is black, they're starting to look like a hurricane, or maybe a big ball of grief. You now hate this color.

Right before you moved in with Heather, you'd heard about a man who lived with his dead mother for almost a year, and you considered what that might be like, to live with your own mother, dead. You smiled at the freedom it would bring. Then you decided that when a person starts thinking about living with a corpse, it must be time to move out. So now you're here.

It's been three months, and you've watched this peculiar cemetery grow for just as long. Heather has admitted to you that she pulls her hair out in the shower and leaves it on the walls. She said it like she expected you to understand this as an accepted truth and, as the person who had just moved in, you'd simply have to deal with it. But you decided you couldn't take it anymore.

You've been biting your nails lately, so your fingers are soft nubs, wrinkled from the water you refuse to leave. You've got a mission. You drag them down the wall, wet hair catching between them, around them, against them, and you pull off every piece that you can. Your hand is gloved in hair, and there is finally a clean space in the shower again.

You get out, a flimsy pink curtain behind you, water still running, your body still dripping wet all over the scummy tiled floor, and you try picking the wet hairs off your hand so you can dispose of them in the little metal trash can next to the toilet. The hairs cling, they stay, they won't move. You pull one off but can't drop it. You try to pull three others but they are stuck. You feel one start cutting off circulation of a finger as you pull, so you spend the next five minutes carefully removing the hair like a surgeon. When you've finished, a new black hole forms in the trash can.

You now know how it feels to take something you've wanted your whole life and destroy it.

You turn off the shower and hear the water trickle down the drain. You don't bother drying off or brushing your hair before you leave the bathroom.

Later that night you buy Clairol hair dye with no ammonia and pick the brightest red you can. You've never wanted red before, but you're feeling risky. You don't know that your base color isn't a dark enough brown to get the full red because you're new to this. Apparently red needs a strong pigment to grab onto. Your hair turns orange. It's degenerate, dry, and dead. Your mother's not dead, and even Heather's loose hair won't die, but the first time you color your hair, it looks like Hell. You consider getting rid of it, like, cutting it all off and adding each strand of your own to the can with Heather's. You think about it, but then you don't. There would be silky black tangled with burnt ginger, and together they might look like Hell's ashes. Something devastating you don't want to look at.

Heather gets home from her job at the dollar store, dragging some boy in a video game graphic t-shirt behind her. She doesn't say anything about your hair. Tomorrow morning when she goes to shower, she won't seem to notice anything missing, but she will begin taking up space again. Ten strands of hair will have returned by the time you use the shower later. When you get out of the shower and wrap yourself in some crummy towel, you'll hear Heather who's styling an updo in the other room say, "Ugh, I hate my fucking hair." The best part is when she adds, "I'm sick of it," and you think, *Me too*.

KEEPING MY SEXUALITY TO MYSELF, THANK YOU VERY MUCH

I HEARD THAT SUSAN FROM work was checking out her butt, touching it and everything, in the bathroom mirror. I guess she didn't realize that her boss was in the stall behind her and saw the whole thing through the stall's crack. Susan swore she was just adjusting a wedgie. I'm not sure if that's true, but either way, I've imagined what kind of underwear she was wearing now.

I'm a woman with low rise lacy underwear, for glamorous holidays like New Years Eve and Valentine's Day, and especially for days worth celebrating, like Fridays and Saturdays. The type of underwear that disappears with the shadows. Screams "bruises on her knees".

I made fun of ladies who wore granny panties made of nylon from Penny's. Simple things that hide their midriff. Women not trying to excite anyone.

But, also, now I'm a Susan from work. One of those women, checking out her butt, rubbing the hills of it in the bathroom mirror, and wondering what kind of underwear the person who catches me thinks I'm wearing.

PERFECT FIT

YOU PLACE YOUR RIGHT HAND'S fingers in a circle around your left wrist. You see how far down your forearm you can go before they must break apart. You find that they can't go far at all, not even one inch. This helps you more accurately picture your weight since you've gained some, and how much of your body might spill out of the lace push-up bra on the rack in front of you if you were to put it on. You decide to buy this one in six months, after you're hopefully done with your diet. If they still stock it then.

A middle-aged woman with brown, blown-out hair, and some outdated navy-blue eyeliner, and a tag on her chest that says her name's Sharon (and she's the owner), asks if you need help. Would you like a dressing room? No thanks, you tell her. You're only looking.

"Looking's great, but imagine wearing it." She winks.

You don't tell her that you already did and that's why you don't need a dressing room.

"Did Hannah put on winged liner for the birth of her child, or did it just happen while she was wearing it?" Another woman who looks like she's in her early twenties says from the register as she flips through a magazine. This one's got naturally red hair, hot pink lips, and a white crop top you can see her bra through.

"She put it on," Sharon says confidently.

And you agree, even though you don't know Hannah.

Sharon turns back to you and says, "You should too."

The other one says, "Yeah, put it on." They aren't talking about eyeliner anymore.

Your hands are touching the set now, and you feel the garment's small petals of lace between your fingers. If scarlet was a texture, it would feel like this, and if sexy was a color, it would look like this. Sharon, closer to you now, puts her unmanicured hand on your back and says, "I don't know if you've gotta special someone at home, but let me tell you somethin', honey—*you* are special enough on your own. You deserve this. I've got an eye for this stuff—you'll look stunning."

"She does have an eye for this stuff," the other one says. She adds, "Here, let me measure you. That way you'll get the best fit." Sharon takes her hand off your back and leaves. The other woman says, "Hi, my name's Tracey. Lift your hands." When you do as she says, Tracey pulls a long, soft measuring tape out of her pocket and loops it behind you then pulls it back around. She tightens it, snug around the top of your rib cage. She leans forward, squints her eyes, and takes note of the number she sees. "Hm," she accidentally says aloud, like she's making a mental note, and then she loosens the tape, raises it higher so it's tight against your boobs, says, "Sorry, I hope this is okay," and she pulls it snug once more to count again.

"Your numbers are thirty-six and thirty-nine," she says finally, as if not to forget them. "This means you are a thirty-six C." You don't know the math problem she did in her head to get this, so you're a little impressed, then you start thinking about how unimpressive that size is.

Tracey peers down at the bra, squints again like she's looking hard at its tag, and she says, "So this one isn't the best fit for you. Try this." She hands you the same set but a little bigger.

"That's okay," you say. You really aren't going to buy it for another six months at best. Think of it as a reward.

"Come on. You can at least try it on."

"Yeah, try it on for me, would ya? It gets a little boring around here this time of day," Sharon adds from behind the cash counter. "Let's just see if I'm right, if this looks stunning on you like I expect."

Tracey smiles as she walks you ten feet to the single dressing room door, revealing a smudge of pink on her front tooth when she smiles. It's particularly noticeable because some of her teeth are more of a white color while some are a little more yellow, and the tooth with the pink is white, which makes it stand out, how embarrassing, but you don't know how to tell her it's there.

Tracey holds the door open for you as you begrudgingly take the hanger from her hand. She shuts it and you lock it, faced with a small space, a mirror nailed to the wall, and your body. You look at yourself and think that your hair is too short. It's not sexy like those girls with beachy waves, and you haven't gotten a proper style in a while. The sweater you're wearing hides any shape you don't like, and you're covered in jewelry, but you like watching your rings follow your reflection.

You turn around to undress yourself, placing each of your clothes in a pile on the floor. With a heavy sigh, you slide your legs through the panties and work on snapping the bra into place.

Like a chorus out in the shop, you hear, "Come on out! Let's see."

You don't look at the mirror as you open the door. You don't leave the dressing room since you're unsure if any customers have come in. You stand there in the door frame, with Sharon and Tracey in front of you, looking up and down your body as if you are some sort of show to be watched.

"It looks like you were made for it," Tracey says through her big, stupid grin. She's got more lipstick on a bottom tooth now.

"No, hun, the phrase is: it was made for you," Sharon corrects Tracey. She adds, directed at you, "But it's true. It looks like it was made for you, girl."

You're about to tell them no, because you know at any second they're going to tell you that you need to get it, and you won't even look at yourself in the mirror.

"Your boobs look great."

You say thanks.

"You know, I mean it when I say it." Sharon puts her hands on her hips. Moves one hand to her chin. Rubs her fingers across her mouth. "Have you ever been a model? I mean, could I get you to be my model?"

"Ooh!" Tracey stands on her tiptoes and claps her hands aggressively.

"Model for what?" You ask. A draft from the air conditioning vent above your head rushes your skin and leaves you covered in goosebumps. You wonder if your nipples are showing but you refuse to look down.

"Model for the store. You know, pictures," she says, and she points to two of the poster frames hanging around the shop with young women in makeup and silky hair, baring their straight, white teeth while in nothing but underwear.

"Oh, no, I couldn't," you say. Because really. You couldn't.

You remember the one time you went on a date at the mall. You guys walked through a bra shop and made-up stories for all the skinny models hanging in frames. You never saw yourself in those stories.

While Tracey starts walking from rack to rack and pulling hangered sets, Sharon explains, "We have promotional campaigns twice a year, and our fall and winter collection will be on sale soon, so I've gotta start promoting it." Her lips curl.

Tracey has a stack of garments hanging over her forearm when she walks back, using her free hand to hold a bra up to you, seeing how it might look. You shake your head. You like the hills of women's shoulders, trailing softly above their collarbones. You like the soft mounds of their flesh, curved around their ribcage and stomach. You like the dip in their hips, pulling your eyes to their panty lines. The way their bodies look like a landscape portrait. So forgiving. So smooth. This is what women in centerfolds and in magazine lingerie ads look like. You don't look like those women though which is why you don't want to do this.

"Really," you say, trying again to tell her no.

Sharon finishes, "Really," thinking she's convinced you. "Are you free two Mondays from now?" Sharon tells you the new sets she's selling are mostly satin and lacy, and she's hoping to get some lifestyle shots. Some robes and French doors, and while she has no French doors because they're shooting here at the shop, she wants to do something to make it look like that. She wants plants, too, real life plants, because they add pizzazz to anything. She asks you what photos you'd like.

"What do you mean?" You ask.

She means, as a model, what would you hope to get out of the shoot?

You shake your head. Your hair is dry and frizzy so it doesn't wag so much as it stays in place, but you don't actually say no. You look over her shoulder at the picture of that runway model in a bikini hanging on the back wall again. You have no intentions to agree to this, but like a reflex, you say, "Sexy pictures," because you bet that model has a million sexy pictures of herself and, wow, how that must feel good. You think you'd love even just one sexy picture of yourself that you might keep in the drawer of your nightstand. Or maybe to show a boyfriend one day. You could say, Hey, look. That's me. I modeled for a lingerie store one time, and you think the man might tell you, Wow. You're so incredibly sexy.

Giving that answer was an accident though. Sharon grins, Tracey still holding bras up against your half-unclothed body, and says, "We can do that for you. We can pay you, too. Doesn't that sound nice?"

Tracey nods her head approvingly at a gold, shimmery bra, with black straps, and says, "Mm. Yes. You look so good."

You don't think that you've ever received these many compliments in your life before. And while you disagree with these women—you think they're absolutely wrong—you don't hate their lies.

"I'm free in two Mondays," you say, knowing very well you're free almost every Monday.

After Sharon tells you that's great, and after she walks to the cash counter to write down some details on a store card, and after she hands you the card she's filled out and says, "We're so excited that you'll represent us. We can't wait to see you back here soon," you take off the set you're wearing. Like you promised, you don't buy what you tried on today.

Tracey tells you to show up hair and makeup ready. "There will be food and fun!"

You are unsure if you regret the decision your shaky self-esteem just made you agree to.

You stood in front of your mirror, curled your hair, brushed it out, pinned it up, took it down, curled it again, used your curling iron to flatten it, put it in a ponytail, and coated your eyelashes with thick mascara. You lined your lips and filled them in with red lipstick. You thought about throwing on a wool jacket because you didn't want to show your shoulders, but then you took a deep breath, told yourself to get it together, and you didn't.

At the store you see four people. Sharon the manager, Tracey the assistant, a man with a professional camera, and another woman whose back faces you. You obviously can't see much of her, but you can already tell that she looks nothing like you.

Tracey notices the bell ring on the door as you open it first. She calls to you, "Welcome! Come on over."

When you walk up next to the new woman, you notice her hair is dyed platinum blonde and her tips are a hot pink. She's missing a plastic nail on her middle finger.

The team turns around, and all of them stare at you. You wave with only your fingers and Sharon breaks into a heavy chuckle, which makes you laugh a little too. Everyone softens. She tells Tracey to grab your sets, and you know the two of them have already undressed you with their eyes. You tell yourself it's all right. This is a good thing, in fact, because if they didn't like what they saw when they did that, then you wouldn't be here.

The new woman holds her hand out to shake yours, and you welcome it. As you touch your palm to hers, she looks you in the eyes and says her name is Valerie.

Tracey pulls your arm straight out and hangs a pile of at least ten garments on it. After she points to the man with the camera and says his name is Steve and he'll be shooting you today, she pushes you toward the dressing room and says to try all of those on. She tells you if you spill out of them a little, it's okay, just make sure it's not too much, and you want to tell her no thanks, because spilling out of anything in a permanent photograph, one hung inside of a professional shop no less, is a nightmare you don't want to play dress up in. Instead you tell her okay and lock the dressing room door.

They've got a stand set up with a long roll of peach paper hanging from it that you hear Steve call a fawn color, and a big light with an umbrella. They've got a potted plant in the corner, but there are no French doors. You hear the photographer begin directing Valerie. You unzip your jeans and notice indentation marks left in their place when you remove them, and you hear him tell Valerie to put her left hand on her hip. Then shake her hair out with her left hand. Then cross her arms but make sure her left hand is tucked away. You realize that her missing nail is on her left hand, so that makes sense.

You've tried on seven sets so far and would only consider buying one that is a champagne color, but Sharon yells to you that you're taking a while. She asks if everything's okay. Yeah, you say, and she says to come out and show them. You did not realize you were supposed to show every single set, so you walk out of the dressing room in the one you're wearing.

"The others are fine," you tell her, and she doesn't ask any questions when she nods her head. Valerie, who's got a big smile and her hands on her hips, looks over at you from where they are shooting in the corner with her in knee-high socks and simply says, "Cute."

You can't tell what that means.

Sharon tells you to come on out if they all work, so you're left standing in a thong next to Sharon and Tracey while you all watch Valerie spin around in a shiny bodysuit. When no one else pays you any more attention, you wonder if they all feel the same way Valerie feels about you, whatever way that is.

Like she's picking up a conversation that must have started earlier, Sharon tells Steve that she was a kid in the eighties, and everything was mental then. She says sixteen-year-old girls would take twenty-four-year-old men to prom and everyone thought it was fine. Steve says that when he was in seventh grade, they made it illegal to smoke in schools and a few teachers nearly walked out. His mom told him she'd smoke and drink all day too if she had the teachers' jobs, so when one of them finally quit, no one was too upset that the kids didn't learn much that year.

After two hours of Valerie flirting with the camera, hiding her left hand, and flipping her hair behind her shoulders to clear her cleavage, Sharon tells everyone to take a lunch break. Small drops of sweat line Steve's forehead. Sharon apologizes to you, says she's sorry and she swears you'll be up next as soon as you all get back.

They said they'd have food for you, and while they didn't lie—there is food—the food is a tray of vegetables and ranch dip that's been sitting out on a card table all day, so by the time it's lunch, they've all gotten warm, and some flies that made it in the front door have begun nesting there.

You walk to the bowling alley down the street to get a personal pizza your roommate raves about. When you open the box on your walk back, you realize you just paid for a personal pizza that's mostly uncooked, the cheese isn't melted, so you take a few bites of the crust and decide maybe this is a sign from somewhere that it's best you don't eat today. After all, you don't want to look bloated for the pictures.

When you get back, Sharon's telling Steve about how when she was really little, her mom would pin a small list and twenty bucks to her shirt and send her and her brother up to the corner liquor store to get their daddy some beer, momma some VA slims, and a box of ice pops. Steve shakes his head and sighs. He says that the world used to be so much more forgiving back then.

You go to put on the first set you're shooting in and hear Sharon call out that you're up. Finally. Tracey and Valerie are missing still, but you prefer less people anyway.

You walk out of the dressing room and feel a little chilly, thanks to the fact that you're mostly naked. Steve points and tells you where to stand. He says he needs a few minutes to adjust the lighting, and you know this is because you're shorter and rounder than Tracey. You've decided that you're the model everyone's supposed to feel sorry for, or good about, because you're more "diverse." If Tracey wasn't missing a plastic fingernail, and if she was a little more graceful, she would be stunning.

You tell yourself to grow up and stop it. You promised yourself that today you'd be sexy.

Steve waves you in the center of his backdrop and says he's testing his light and settings now so you can just stand there for a minute. You do as he asks and fold your arms firmly across your chest while you wait for further directions. The cotton panties start to rub against your thighs and you almost reach down to scratch.

When he's finished pushing buttons, he looks up like he's really noticing you for the first time. You watch his eyes scan you up, then down, and he says, "Flirt for me."

You think of the one centerfold picture you had growing up. The woman grabbed her butt with one hand and a tit with the other so you go ahead and slide one hand down and one hand up. Steve says nothing about how you cover the garments and instead he tells you to turn around and bend forward a little. He says, "Look back over your shoulder and wink." He takes a few shots like this and you cannot tell if it's because you look sexy or untamed. Does it matter?

Valerie and Tracey walk in, laughing over something, but Valerie stops to watch your movements. She has to know they've all been directed and cannot blame you too much for how you look.

Sharon says, "Wait a minute, she should change into her next look." Steve shrugs and you leave to switch out your set.

When you get back, Steve tells you to get on your knees. The hard floor hurts but you stay like that for at least three minutes as he walks you through multiple variations of one pose. First it's knees with hands up, smiling. Then it's knees with hands crossed below the bra to accentuate your cleavage. Then it's hands on the ground and you're on all fours like something feral. After a while, you stop noticing the way Steve keeps you down, because you like how he looks from above. Hair has fallen across your face but when you go to tuck it back behind your ears, Steve says to keep it there and close your eyes. Now open your mouth a little. You do as you are told because you like what you've turned into. You think about how you've wanted to feel this way your whole life.

Valerie gives you a whistle. She cries out, "Get it!" You try not to blush, but Steve tells you to lean into it. He says it's cute and people love a cute girl.

You think you hear Valerie ask someone when it's her turn, she still has five other sets to model, but it's hard to tell through Steve's directions.

He tells you to put on the next bra, which is one that looks more like a bow on a Christmas gift. He says, "Perfect," when you're back in front of the camera and he shoots you tucking your hair behind your ears.

"Yeah?"

He repeats, "Yeah. You're perfect."

You want more than anything for it to be true, and by the end of your sets, you almost think it might be.

When Sharon tells you in a little bit that that's it, you're done, and now Valerie can finish up, Valerie walks past you kneeling on the floor and whispers, "You know he's using you. They all are." She has a little bit of lipstick smeared above her lip like Tracey and you do not tell her.

As you're still sitting on the floor, you ask Valerie towering over you how it's any different from her. You two are doing the same job, after all. Valerie rolls her eyes.

She says, "I'm used to it."

Like being used to it changes what it is or something. It doesn't.

"Is that what you want?"

Valerie shrugs. Her hair tousled gently on her shoulders, she lifts her hands up to brush it off so it falls perfectly straight again. Her response is, "Is that what *you* want?"

"Valerie!" Steve shouts over his shoulder and you watch her firm ass, wrapped in a pair of hip hugger panties, wiggle as she leaves you behind. Steve starts directing her into poses that mirror the ones he made you do.

Tracey, who was behind the cash counter, now comes toward you and thanks you for your hard work today. She says,

"You're exactly what we needed. I can't wait to see your photo up around the store."

"Sure."

Tracey hands you a plastic gift card that has the shop name and some bra clip art printed on it. You roll it over in your hand. Scratched in permanent marker is *$100* on the back. "This is how we pay you. Feel free to get something you tried on today, or anything else you'd like here."

You thank her and take the card, but you still don't want any of this, so you stick it in your pocket for another day.

The flash goes off. Steve says, "Yes—give it to me."

There are pictures of other models hanging above the door as you leave.

You imagine your body like a landscape portrait, black and white, framed and hanging. Other women coming to buy something their men will undress them from, will look at your flesh like the rolling hills of somewhere no one lives. You hope Steve crops out identifying features, like your face or your hips, or maybe just not use the photos at all. Maybe they can just use Valerie. Maybe that would be what everyone expects, and maybe that is all right.

HUNGER

I HEAR HER UNLEASH IT in the end stall, see her knees on the ground. The toilet water goes splash, and then the reverse-cough like she's releasing all the evil inside her. At some point she starts to sound empty. I don't even know who she is.

I'm in the girl's bathroom next to the cafeteria, washing my hands in cold water and drying them off with the crunchy paper towel, pulling the knob down aggressively so it makes more noise. I don't know if I do it to be comforting so she feels less exposed, or so I don't have to hear her that loud.

I toss the paper towel in the trash can and use the mirror to swipe on one more coat of my Strawberry Sundae Lip Smacker and go back to class. I can't stop thinking about the girl though, and how I've never heard her do that before. I wonder if it's her first time, or if she's a pro. I wonder what goes through her mind when she does it. I wonder what she sees when she looks in the mirror. I wonder what she sees when she looks at me.

I get home and put on more lip balm. I get really close to the mirror this time to make sure I make the perfect shape on my lips. Then I realize that the shape I make doesn't matter, because I will ruin it anyway. Whatever. I still try.

My mom has a pile of clothes she's donating to the thrift store because they don't fit her anymore. She told me last night I should go through my clothes too. She said we could all use some updated wardrobe. She doesn't know that I've had a pile ready for months.

Amy asked how I was feeling last week. *Bloated?* She said my clothes looked kinda tight. *No offense.* She's not wrong, but it's only because I stole this pair of jeans to replace the clothes in my pile, and they are a size smaller than I am right now. They are encouragement.

I hear that girl throw up again, every time I go to the bathroom. Every time I look in the mirror. Every time I squeeze into my skinny jeans. I hear her purge when I watch the women on television, and when I look at the calories on the back of my cereal box before I eat. My mom notices me looking at them, and I tell her I'm reading the company's brand story. She says that's nice and I say, Yeah, but I don't want any milk today.

I start skipping lunch. It gives me more time to talk with Ashley and Sarah at the table since they also don't eat. It takes Ron and Nicole forever to come back from the line, so I barely get to talk to them by the time they're done with their Bosco Sticks and chocolate milk. I watch the cheese stretch between the bread and Nicole's mouth, and have to play the girl's purge in my head to keep myself from reaching across the table to practically take the strand out of Nicole's mouth.

I tell Mom I'm walking home after school. We don't live too far, and it'll save her the trip. Even though she says I don't have to do that, I can tell she's relieved. Since we live in a neighborhood just a half mile from school, I take the long way and walk in squares around all the blocks instead of a straight-line home.

After a while, two girls ask me what I've been doing to look so good. I ask them what they mean even though I can't stop smiling. I shrug them off and tell them I don't know what they are talking about. They whisper down the hall, and I even see one look back over her shoulder at me. I watch them walk into the bathroom, one after the other, like it is a party in there or something, and I wonder if they've ever heard the girl. Or any other girls.

Then the spring formal arrives and even though I've spent three weeks picking out my dress and hair and makeup, I don't want anyone to think I'm trying too hard, so I don't tell them. Theresa says that Rob wants to ask me out, she says he asked her how I'd want him to, and when I ask her what she told him, she says she had no clue how I'd like it. She said I'd probably be happy either way. And yeah, even if I've dreamt of a boy standing outside the locker room after gym class with a poster painted red, or a punk kid giving me a cookie at lunch with my name written in frosting, she isn't wrong. I would be happy either way. Rob never does ask me though, but I take it as a sign. I'm holding out for Kenny, and I realize I shouldn't eat a cookie anyway.

When I try on my dress in front of my bedroom mirror, it is a little too big, and that makes me run my hands over my straightened curves religiously. At school the next day, Gavin talks to me in first hour even though he's never talked to me before. Then it's two days out from the dance and Jeremy asks me what my favorite movie is. I think I see him check me out before he asks. At least I hope that's what happened. Otherwise I'm stuck worrying that I'm still too big. Still too unimpressive. Still too imperfect. I will always be too something.

I draw pictures of Kenny. In my English notebook, behind fake summaries of novels I've never read. In my agenda, on pages where I don't list the homework I should've done. I draw one of Kenny and me holding hands on the back of a napkin from lunch that I put in my purse because I know I want to tape it to my mirror when I get home. I've had a crush on him for a while. We don't have a class together, but our fourth hour classes are right next to each other, so I walk past him every day. There is one day left till the dance, and I tell my friends I have a quiz to make up for Mr. Wilson during lunch, so I walk laps around the school instead, mostly passing Kenny's class, trying not to make it obvious when I look in the small window next to the door to see him writing some sort of note. Who is it to?

No one asks me to the dance, so I get myself ready, pinning the loose fabric of my A-line dress back, and curling my hair not too tight, and putting on eyeliner so my eyes look smokey, but not so dark that I look like I'm dying, and I go with my best friend, but only because I didn't get a date. Her dress is too tight for her figure, but I tell her she looks cute when I get in her mom's car.

When we get to the gym full of balloons, and I see Alyssa with her hair straightened and teased, and her lips so bright she could be another disco light on the dance floor, I feel humiliated I haven't done more. No one will notice me like this. So when we've spent at least forty minutes with the DJ in the gym, with mostly no boys around, and it is just me and a few other girls enjoying each other's company (like Jade who's even smaller than me), I think about Kenny, where he is, and if he even came. Then I think about the girl in the bathroom and decide to go there myself. I hope to see him waiting, maybe for me, on the edge of the dance floor when I return. As I leave, I pass Trisha who is no bigger than a size two, and Georgia who's probably about the same size as Trisha, and then Rachael who's in a very tight dress and a size zero at her biggest. I wonder if any of them are the girl from the stall.

I'm ten feet from the bathroom and pulling out my lip balm when Jordan, closing a nearby locker, says hey to me and I say hey back. He's got on a hot pink tie and white Converse that he's drawn all over, and he smiles a goofy, lopsided smile at me. I can't help but smile too. He asks how my night's going so I stop to tell him it's all right. He says, Yeah, same here. He asks what I've been up to lately and then my favorite song starts playing behind me, out on the dance floor. I turn to look and he notices. I tell him how I love Daughtry's 'It's Not Over,' and then wonder if I've just embarrassed myself, but he asks me if he could make the song even better. I'm not sure how, but I tell him sure, and then he gently pushes me against the wall of lockers and kisses me. He runs his hand from my shrinking hips up to the bottom of my too-small boobs. He presses against my lips harder. My tube of lip balm falls to the floor.

I think of my best friend and how Jordan is *her* crush. I think of all the drawings of him hanging on her mirror that he doesn't know about. I hope he doesn't move his hand behind me or he'll feel the pins. I kiss back harder, hoping he knows that this means something to me, because this is the first time a boy's ever kissed me to start. I've never really thought of Jordan this way before, but now I am. Over his shoulder I see my best friend watching me from the dance floor. I imagine the picture she's seeing and wonder what this would look like if she drew it. She's a much better artist than me—I bet it would look good, at least, especially since I'm thinner now. But she might realize that and decide to get skinny too. All the girls might. I mean, there's nothing keeping them from discovering my secrets and doing them as well, and then I'll be left behind… so when Jordan finally pulls away from me, still looking kind of eager, I can't help but wonder how long this will last.

STOLEN NAMES

WE'RE IN THE GUEST BATHROOM cutting our hair like we're shedding something of ourselves. I've got a fistful of Andi's in one hand and industrial shears in the other as we face the mirror. Some toothpaste spit fogs the reflection a little, but otherwise I can see us head-on. Like we're clear. For the longest time, before this moment, it had mostly been me and her, but then she tells me in a fake-diamond type of way that she's thinking about how nice it'd be if our parents got married, because then the loneliness would all be over. We'd be real sisters. A loose piece of her hair falls somewhere on my skin. I stand above her sitting on the toilet as she imagines this other world where Dad and I need someone, but she's wrong. We don't need anyone stealing our names. The back of Andi's neck feels tender from how often she uses conditioner. I stroke it with my thumb as we stare at ourselves, looking at who we are. I ask her if she's ready, but before she says anything, I slice her long hair in half. The cut's not straight. Her mouth splits into a snarl that looks the same as the cut I just made, and I drop all of her wiry ends on the floor. Sometimes she forgets things are temporary, so she's screaming, like some wild animal, that with hair like this now, she'll always be alone and, I don't know, maybe she's right. Or maybe we all will.

BOYS MAKE THE SAME MISTAKES

"THERE WAS A BOY I kissed once, my first kiss, thirteen, in his mother's basement circled by a group of mutual friends."

Stacey asks me if it was for a game of spin the bottle.

Yeah.

Bent over my face, she says, "It always is." Her hot breath on top of me.

I add, "But I thought I might want it, to do it. I had never done it before—kiss a boy."

I'm wearing jeans and a big pullover hoodie, but still feel naked with my first kiss on show and tell. Stacey's got me lying on her kitchen floor made of olive-green linoleum with some design that looks like it belongs stamped on a genie's bottle.

I tell her, "There were six of us, crowded in that little half-finished space, but somehow still spread out, like stretched telephone wires. I don't think it was his first time, I mean, I'm pretty sure he'd kissed girls before, at least *a* girl maybe, I don't know how many. I'm sure I knew at the time, but it's hard for me to remember now, all these years later. And I think back to that moment, how one kiss seemed like such a big deal, how we were facing each other, surrounded by friends, and so many freckles constellated his nose, I still remember that at least, and how I put my hands on his knees instead of mine when I finally leaned in to kiss him."

"Finally?"

I tell her, "Time felt like eternity."

Stacey asks what that feels like.

"When they all shoved me in the middle and told me to kiss him, they felt like friends and strangers all at once. I was swallowed by sweat, but then I leaned in, forehead to forehead, and he pressed his lips against mine. Soft. Maybe. Hard and awkward. I try to remember but I can't. It's okay, I guess. A first kiss is a first kiss, what's it matter anyway?"

Stacey says, "Right." She asks, "You doin' okay?"

I've had my eyes closed this entire time, but it doesn't help me picture the memory.

This isn't the first tattoo Stacey has given, so she has touched girls before. She knows the way their bodies are impressionable and leave imprints when pushed against. She knows what makes those imprints. Vulnerability doesn't scare her.

She presses the tattoo gun against the soft skin of my cheek. She looks straight at my face, like maybe she's searching it for something, but I don't think she finds anything. She carries on with redesigning me. I consider opening my eyes, but understand it's best not to until everything is over.

"Beauty is pain, right?" I finally answer. I've heard this statement many times in my life. I'm just repeating it.

"That's what they say." Above the gun's buzz, she adds, "But I've got your boyhood story beat. I've got the silhouette of a small Pit Bull on my wrist." My eyes are still closed, so I can't see it, and with her gun still against my cheekbone, I don't dare to speak. She continues, "My man's name was Dave Barkley." She says, "Get it? Bark-ley. Bark. Bark like a dog barks."

My cheeks are the color of a soft berry and feel like they're on fire.

She says that he took her to get the tattoo. They were both young, although she was younger than him, and on the way to his brother's to get the tattoo, he convinced her it would show their love which, she says that she realizes now, was a funny way of saying labelling, which is what it really was. "I didn't know then that ten other girls, and by girls, I mean *girls*—like younger-than-seventeen *girls*—had the same tattoo."

She's finished with my cheeks and moves the gun above my eye. She finds the spot she's looking for and I feel it press against me, waiting.

"My best friend Janae and I went to the ice cream shop up our block. It was summertime in, like, tenth grade, I think. I knew Dave for five months, and then got the tattoo—I know, but five months was huge in tenth grade. I was head-over-heels for him, like, talkin' Janae's ear off about him head-over-heels. We went inside the shop, and then I stopped dead in my tracks when it was our turn to order. The girl on the other side of the counter couldn't have been more than, like, sixteen, I swear—I recognized her from the other school I would've gone to if I lived one more mile up the road—and we had matching tattoos."

The drilling above my eye has started to give me a headache.

"I found out about the other nine when that girl told me. I stopped her cute little *hello*, smiley, *what do you wanna order* crap and asked where she got the dumb tattoo. Demanded to know why. I felt like a sister wife or some shit after she told me, so I didn't order ice cream that day. Walked right out. I don't know how many others he *got*, I mean *convinced*, after me. It's a number I'll never know."

Stacey stops her gun. The straight tips of two perfect eyebrows are fixed above my eyes.

To keep the pain down, I move my lips minimally when I say, "So the dog's still there?" My lips are the shape and color of rose petals now, forever kissable.

"I told you it was."

"Why didn't you remove it or hide it? You're covered in tattoos. It must've been easy to hide a tiny little dog."

"It's a part of my story. Just like the rest."

"The rest... of the other girls? With tattoos? Other boys? Who... you kissed?"

"The rest of my tattoos. So it stays."

Stacey smears leftover ink away, leaving what probably looks like a bruise around the new pretty that's permanently covering my face. A real bruise will most likely take its place for the next week before it heals.

After thinking for a minute, Stacey goes, *Hmm*. She says, "I bet you were embarrassed, because didn't you still like his friend?"

She hands me a small mirror so I can finally see myself. I watch my mouth say, "What?" to her.

"You mentioned earlier that, in that basement, you liked one guy but ended up kissing the other. The boys were friends, right? I'm just saying, that musta been embarrassing, kissing some boy in front of the one you really liked."

"Oh. Does it matter? I think he might've been embarrassed too. Who knows who he liked."

BERRIES, BLOOD, WHEAT

ON ANOTHER SIDE OF THE world, some girl is dancing by herself on a crowded floor, with spotlights kissing her body. But here I am, waking up in a quilted bed, thinking, *Berries, blood, wheat.* I don't know what it means, but I can't stop thinking it. It just sounds like something I should remember.

It's early in the morning—too early—but I walk naked through the dark to the kitchen where I drench my face in faucet water. I let it pour over me as my head hangs beneath it. My hair dark and sloppy. I am wearing nothing but my skin, stretched and scarred from time.

I choke on the excess, water dripping from my mouth with each cough, as I walk to the living room, framed by the house's front window. I should've bought blinds for it, but I didn't. I figured it's near impossible to see in here anyway with how the house sits on a small incline above the street, so I never got them.

A red landscaping truck drives past my house, with a man in a yellow vest at the wheel, and for a moment I think he sees me standing here in nothing. I realize how improbable this is and don't move. I should leave, should not stay here, but instead I watch the same truck drive past again because it must've turned around, and then just moments later, it drives by a third time, in the direction it had been going originally.

I heard my first catcall as a child. My neighbor Kathy and I were little girls playing dolls on her porch. She had one with long, shiny hair and a fairy princess dress. I had a regular doll. I don't remember the kind. The old man stopped before walking by and whistled. I think he was married. He wore a gold band. Kathy whistled back and laughed. I hadn't learned how to whistle yet but I wished I could. I wanted him to notice me and my sound too. The man smiled at us, and in a voice like western gravel, he said we were special. Kathy's mom yelled from the kitchen—we could hear through the screen door that it was supper time. The sun was setting. The man left, and although I knew that I'd never see him again, I would never forget him.

I cannot tell what the man driving by now is looking at in the dark, but I wonder if he's looking at me. If I was an eleven-year-old girl, I'm sure he'd look closer.

I wait a little longer, my fourteen-year-old daughter asleep in her room, but the man does not return. If I had curtains, I might shut them. If I think about it, I might not. When I'm convinced the man is truly gone, I leave the window. I can't help but think, *Berries, blood, wheat.*

WHAT A MEMORY LOOKS LIKE

THEY DIDN'T EVEN LAY HER embalmed body out in a casket for us to see like I wanted. Instead they put her ashes in a thrift store mixing bowl. Nearly forty percent of people get put in caskets, and they're placed in a mausoleum, or buried in a cemetery, but not my sister. The bowl is barely big enough to hold her, but it has some nice little roses painted on the side, so Ma thinks it works just fine.

Ma stands at the front door of the VFW Hall where she's ushering people into my sister's memorial. She has started thinking that the helium balloons she roped outside might scream party and not memorial, so she's freaking out, worried that people might miss it. I don't expect many people today anyway though.

Ma laughs and says, "Yeah, yeah, we're lucky they brought Chicken Shack. Here's a pack of cigarettes we can all share. Watch that pothole on your way in so you don't twist your ankle," as my second cousin walks past her. She hands him an already half-empty pack and points at the folding table set up with some tin pans and fried chicken. The scent is faint, but a whiff of some fryer oil and butter can still be caught from the right angle.

There's maybe fifteen people standing around, staring at the oily meat. I tell her that we're half past the time the invites said we were going to start, and she says sure, just give her five more minutes. I ask how many people she's expecting, and she responds, "Good lord, this is your sister. Can't you have a little respect?"

When her five minutes are up and no one else comes in, Ma walks to her cousin, grabs the lit cigarette straight from his mouth and hooks it in her own lips, inhaling it the best she can. Her ma, my grandma, stands to her right and though I can't hear what Grandma says, I figure she asks for her share of the cig because Ma unwillingly hands it to her and they keep passing it back and forth until it's burnt to nothing.

Dad stands up and ushers the small group to quiet down. The lights are dim, the walls are a faded cream, and the ceiling's brown. Dad's next to Elizabeth's bowl and a posterboard of pictures and the first thing he says is, "God is good."

Ma says loud enough so that everyone can hear, "Couldn't more of his congregation come?"

"Maryann, would you cut it out? I'm delivering my daughter's eulogy."

"Listen, I'm just saying, doesn't your church even like you? They can't come out for your daughter?"

Dad snarls like a hyena facing its prey. He stands his ground.

Things to know about my father: he is a man who is balding (but keeps the crown of wispy, brown hair around his scalp instead of shaving it off), he is a man who only dresses up when he has to, and he tells it like it is. So he says, "Maryann, shut your ass up, this is our daughter's memorial and you're being an awful host."

Ma pulls the second-to-last cigarette from the pack and lights it since she's already removed all the smoke detectors. She puts it in her mouth and does exactly as Dad tells her to.

I don't listen to most of what he says because it's long and dull, and it won't bring her back. I look at the cracks between the concrete blocks in the wall instead. Dad ends on, "He has made everything beautiful."

I guess the other thing to know about my father is that he's a preacher who shows off God when it's convenient for him.

The crowd does a Hail Mary that I don't follow, then Ma stands up and claps her hands. She gives her spitty cigarette to Grandma and says, "All right, everyone—it's time to eat! We've got Chicken Shack here, grab a plate, have a seat, and let's remember our little girl as she was."

Ma uses "little girl" facetiously. My sister was twenty-one.

I was eighteen and in our basement on a school night. Everything was dark, except the floor lamp above the little side table I was sitting in front of. My sister was twelve, and she came down the stairs with a pile of t-shirts and sweatpants for the wash. I know I said *shit* and tried to wipe everything up, but she saw it anyway and asked what I was doing. I didn't answer her at first—what was I supposed to tell her? Then she asked if it was coke, and I had to tell her yeah.

So that girl sat down next to me and asked if she could try some. I remember thinking about it, and since I hadn't been much older than her when I first tried it, I said fine. I told her just a little because that's all I had left and I wasn't sure when I'd be getting more.

She looked like a puppy dog waiting for a treat, which made me wonder how long she had wanted to try coke for. I didn't ask her though, and instead I told her she should put her hair up because it was long and stringy and going to hang down when she tried to snort and I didn't want to hold it for her. I gave her my hair tie which she used to put her hair into some messy bun.

Elizabeth was a natural. She barely needed directing which almost offended me a little because I'd been doing coke for nearly five years, but whatever.

I guess I don't know how much she enjoyed it that first time because she wasn't one to tell me what she thought or felt, and with me being eighteen, I think that made her even more nervous. You don't want to look dumb when you're twelve.

I get in the back of the line, which isn't a very long line, but the short wait is noteworthy because the old woman in front of me is wiping tears off her cheeks and smearing black, inky makeup on her palms. They look like the ink from those inkblot tests, like two empty faces staring at me.

The table is set up next to three poster boards duct taped to the cinder block wall. There's my sister with a smile plastered between her cheeks. She's a naked toddler in a bathtub because it's adorable or something. She's got a smirk on because it's prom, but she's not going so she's dressed in a black tank top, cutoff jeans, and a row of elastic bracelets that look like bangles while she stands with four friends in suits and floor length gowns. They are going to leave her behind once the photo's taken. I don't know who put these memories together.

I think about eating cheesy potatoes next to a dead girl's ashes, but I guess living people still gotta eat. I've never been to a memorial with food before, but I tell the cousin next to me I know it's customary for many regions and religions to do something like this. She doesn't say anything back.

At the start of the table, I reach past a young man to grab a fork and plate. He lets me, and then I start picking at a chicken tray with tongs before he says, "Honey barbeque, right?"

I tell him I think so. I pick through different flavored chicken wings, almost rainbow-colored as far as chicken goes.

He grabs another set of tongs from the tray and says, "Here, smell it," and sticks a fat piece of chicken in my face before dropping it down his white button up. He's one of the nicest dressed people in here so I laugh. He leaves the chicken on the floor and puts a second one on his plate.

"What's your name?" He asks as he puts macaroni salad next to his maybe-honey-barbeque-but-not-really-sure chicken wings. "How old are you? How come I've never met you before?"

I absentmindedly tell him I've been gone for a while.

"Where are you sitting?" He continues as I add a sprinkled donut to the edge of my plate.

"With my family."

The man looks me up and down one more time.

"Oh, well, I'll see you before you leave then."

I ended up at my friend Joe's place one Friday night. He invited a bunch of friends, so it was one of those laid-back type of parties where we were all sitting around together, shooting the shit. It wasn't a party party with music and people you didn't know, or things like that. He was older than me by two years and had his own place.

Hope had a car, so she picked Kane up, who got shotgun, and then me, who was stuck in the back. Kane had just gotten his first tattoo. It was a snake on his forearm, and he was so excited that he wore a short sleeve shirt in December with snow on the ground so he could show it off. He was the first in the group to get a tattoo. He told us his mom didn't know, so we couldn't say anything to her, as if we would, but his friend's brother gave it to him. I saw Hope roll her eyes in the rearview mirror at me, so I made a gagging face back.

At the party, she pulled out a marker and started writing the names of all the boys around us on my jeans. Dan asked if he could write his own name, so I let him, and by the end of the night, my jeans were nearly black, covered in names and hearts so indistinguishable that I didn't know who any of them were anymore. Alyssa, who showed up late, noticed Dylan's name on my thigh and asked why it was there. I told her Hope was just writing boys' names, but Alyssa was pissed. I knew she had dated Dylan, but I also knew that she hadn't even wanted to date Dylan. I didn't think she knew that we had hooked up after they broke up, but maybe she did. She was so upset I wrote his name down that she got up and left immediately. We started writing on Hope's jeans.

It was after midnight that Hope drove us back to my place and we found the ambulances in the driveway.

Our table looks like the VIP section, front row seats, next to the photo boards.

I sit down next to Ma who's already halfway through her food. She piles it on her fork and shoves the small mountain in her mouth, chewing so loud we all know how much she's eating. She swallows and starts the process all over again.

When Dad sits down beside me, he has to tuck a napkin in his shirt to hide a wet stain he's already gotten on his chest. He's never careful with his food and clothes so he looks sort of funny.

Ma looks up and then waves her hand at us. She says, "Girl, get closer to your dad." She pulls a thin Kodak digital camera from her purse and hands it to a woman with an eye patch next to her, someone I don't recognize. Middle-aged women must have an unspoken understanding about the importance of memories because Ma doesn't even ask the lady a question. Instead, she walks around the table, huddles between me and Dad, wrapping her arms around our shoulders, posing, and the woman just knows what to do.

The woman holds it up against her good eye. She lightly presses the button so the lens focuses.

"Excuse me?" I ask Ma.

My sister is bouncing on a teeter totter next to us. She is learning how to skateboard to our left. She is laughing with her friends on eighth grade graduation day, jewels glued on graduation caps and Lisa Frank stickers on their hands, which wasn't *too* long ago.

"Smile, guys," Ma says as she puts her arm around me.

"Look, Ma, I don't think this is the —"

She smacks my back. She says, "Smile!" And I manage a gag before the woman takes a photo.

Ma reaches across the table for the camera, and when the woman tells her we didn't smile, the next thing Ma does is moan.

"Why?" She asks us.

I tell her that memorials aren't a JC Penny's. No one said they were good places for family portraits.

My sister smirks from behind her fifth birthday cake, and in another she growls through the brown, painted, fake-fur mane of her favorite Halloween costume. She swims on the beach and stands in front of boys who have their arms wrapped around her in a few other photos too. My sister waves to me in the one and only photo we have of her holding the puppy she hid from our parents for a week in another. We're still not sure what happened to that pup after Ma caught us with it in the closet and told us Dad was taking it to live a good life down at the river.

Dad found Elizabeth on her bed, with a sweaty fever, throwing up in her trash bucket. He called the ambulance, and I'm honestly surprised he did because he won't usually let anyone else get involved in our business. The medics were pulling Elizabeth out on that wheely cart when me and Hope had pulled up, and I stayed behind when Ma drove off with them. Elizabeth never told me where she got the coke from that time. I had no idea she was doing it on her own. I had figured she'd been safe doing it the whole time because she had me helping her. Until she didn't.

When she came home the next day, I went ahead and yelled at her, like, full on bellows. I knew she'd heard it enough from the doctors and our parents and stuff, but I told her she needed to listen to me. Like, I didn't want her doing that by herself. So we waited until Ma and Dad left, and then did a line in the living room to celebrate her survival—what a fucking accomplishment.

Ma's finished with her plate and stands up to throw it out. Before walking away, she pats the woman with the eyepatch on the back as a sort of thank you. Not quietly, Ma says to the woman that cocaine's a hell of a drug that's taking too many damn lives. The woman agrees and says they need to get it off the street. She says they should arrest the people out here who give it away like candy. They're the real criminals. Ma nods her head and leaves the table. Dad has barely touched his food. He looks up at me and asks if I remember back when I used to steal Elizabeth's baby toys and give them away. He said I must've been seven or so, but I don't remember. I ask him if he has any proof of this and he says he guesses not. He just remembers things going missing for no reason and having to go out to get replacements.

I remember Taylor, who had a sister two years older. Taylor took some of her sister's earrings and traded them with me for my posts that she wanted. Her sister had big gold hoops, and

I had enough posts, so I didn't mind giving some away. I never even wore the hoops more than once.

I'm sure my dad's right about things going missing, but I don't know if it was because of me. I really don't remember taking baby toys, and I don't know who I'd have given them to, or why I'd want to.

Dad gets up to toss his plate too. He passes the last photo board which has more recent pictures of Elizabeth. An Elizabeth I barely knew. I got out of prison for getting caught with my own cocaine, like, five years ago, and hadn't talked to her much since then. She had since gotten her own friends, and they did their own things.

There's a picture of her at a party with black and green balloons floating against the ceiling. She's got a red plastic cup and some man is kneeling, tying her shoe. In another, she's eating a cheese stick, hugging a dog that looks more like a bear. Someone's finger was in the way so half the photo is dark pink. Then she's surrounded by wall mirrors, holding a mic, singing. In a bar? In someone's basement? She's standing there by herself, except for her own reflection that surrounds her.

I stay seated for a while longer as some sort of bystander. Ma's talking with her hands, back with her second cousin. Dad's wrapping up the food and my grandmother's swatting his arms, trying to stop him from putting it away so soon. Cigarette smoke hangs above the crowd, although I'm unsure where it's coming from anymore. I remember parties like this, when Elizabeth and I were younger. I can't remember when the last one was.

I pass Ma and Dad and the man who's never seen me before (and will never see me again), and a few other people still eating their Chicken Shack. I wonder what photos of them make up their own lives. I wonder if the photo that I just took with Ma and Dad will get put on my own board.

I get to the door with balloons outside it. There's one last picture of Elizabeth when she was three, framed and sitting on a foldable metal chair next to the post with the balloons. In the photo, she's sitting on the living room floor, smiling wide, as I stand behind her. I'm fixing a pink-ribbon bow in her hair because it's come undone. We look young and sweet, but it's not real. I remember Ma taking the picture right before Elizabeth turned to slap me away. She said I was ruining it and she didn't want my help.

I don't say goodbye. I know they'll argue about why I left, whether or not I cared that Elizabeth died, but it isn't about that. When I leave, I am still thinking of all the things I remember about Elizabeth. All the things I remember but will never see again because they weren't captured in photos or put on poster boards. Then, as I start to walk away, I remember what Ma said and make sure I don't trip in the pothole.

LIKE YOU'VE BEEN SITTING AROUND, WAITING, FOR TEN YEARS

JESSICA CALLED LAST WEEK. SHE said Jordan's been asking about you. She said that he told her he's ready to finally date you now, that he just had to grow up. You couldn't help but shudder. You haven't even thought about that boy in ten years. If you had, you would have remembered his laugh—heavy and explosive, erupting when he talked to the other boys about the things he could destroy. You would have remembered his gaze—targeted in the way that was fatal to a girl, something boys could never understand. But wait, no. You would have mostly remembered his approach— no safety, perpetually triggered, and yet effortlessly smooth. Inflicting damage. So you laughed at Jessica through the phone and wondered if she could feel the recoil. You told her that's ridiculous and you hoped she knew that. She said, "I'm shrugging at you right now," and you took that as a sign of disapproval, like maybe she thought it'd be worth trying to date Jordan after all this time, but you wondered in what world it would make sense—to date a man who was once a boy who was nothing more than a firearm.

POURING PERFUME

TILTING GEOMETRIC GLASS BOTTLES UPSIDE down so one-hundred-dollar perfume streams out. Surrounded by tangerine, pomegranate, pulp. Who does this woman think she is? Then brown bottles, warm with gold rims and balm that smells like wood, violin strings, classic. I pour, I smash, I listen to each bottle split into shards I'll leave on the curb at the end of the driveway. I will store their leftover bodies in the sewer where I drop them. A little boy walks by and his nose folds up, wrinkled. He says, "Hello," through his furrowed face. He stops to repeat himself. "Hello." I swivel my legs so the last drops of perfume don't hit my skin. The little boy says, "Goodbye," and I understand. I've become good at goodbyes. Distracted by the boy, I force the last bottle into the ground with a strength I can't seem to control, a splinter thrust in my finger. I pick it out with my teeth, fresh blood on my tongue. I spit the drops down the sewer too. They disappear immediately. I don't understand how she doesn't realize what I'm doing, my stepmother. She asks the household where her perfume goes. My dad tells her he doesn't know. I say, Weird,

I just saw them. And actually, Dad really doesn't know, but he doesn't buy her new bottles anyway. I can't tell if it's boys, men, or self who have been hurting women all along, although it might not matter. I stare at the puncture left on the tip of my finger. The way the blood keeps surfacing. I stop trying to lick it off because I realize it will keep returning.

IT TOOK TONIGHT

YOU STOLE ALCOHOL, SCARRED YOUR skin, and snuggled her neck, and although that was years ago, you can't stop thinking about it now. About Roman, and how she was the sharp, low-to-the-ground hunt of a crocodile. A breath held under water. A mask of day-crust mud. Tonight, you're sitting at a small and wobbly wooden table in front of the little platform stage in the back of the bar when you think of telling Julia about your old friend Roman. You can't tell if she'd care.

Julia returns from the sign-up table and says, "Get ready!" when she sits down next to you. She smiles the way she does when she's drunk and then turns to face the stage.

There was a time when Roman could remove you from yourself and leave behind a kill, an open-casket eulogy.

Julia takes a sip from her drink. Some Guinness she thinks is both bitter and sweet. She ordered you one too, said you'd love it, and you should try something different than usual. You told her you would, although you haven't yet.

Julia says, "So… want some change for the machine with the rubbers?" There's a metal dispenser hanging in the women's restroom next to the busted, swinging door. She laughs loudly at herself and taps your arm. You like how Julia wears lip gloss and a ponytail. You think the fake eyelashes are too much, and maybe the way she laughs too. You shake your head.

You say to her, "I'm not going to need them."

"Sure you will. After all of these men see you up there on stage, they won't be able to keep their hands off you."

The bar is full of the men she's talking about. Long or short pepper-colored hair, scruffy chins, and anchor tattoos on their tanned, flabby biceps. You imagine their thick fingers gripping the plains of your body, their breath pooled in the dimples they leave behind, their overwhelming shadows pressed against you, on top of you.

"I don't think so."

A man at a table behind you says, "You gonna get up there and sing to us? Look all pretty?" You turn when you hear him talk. You see an olive-colored t-shirt that says Big Bass on it, and he smiles a gummy smile. He adds, "Lucky me. I got some change to toss your way." He waves a flimsy dollar at you.

Julia blinks her long black lashes at him, her gold hoops jiggling as she laughs.

Roman promised you once that you two would go sing karaoke together, but it never happened. Now it's seven years later and you're at a bar that has karaoke with Julia. You decide it's best not to tell her about Roman.

A man in a white t-shirt, cracked leather vest, and a silver beard down to his chest calls some lady named Sarah up on stage. You don't know Sarah. She has two piercings in each ear and you think about how she might have pierced them herself with a needle when she was young. This woman doesn't look as old as most of the people in this bar do, she might be around Julia's age, but this realization makes you understand that you are definitely the youngest.

The man up front says, "Sarah's going to sing the classic 'Baby One More Time,'" and the men in the bar whoop. The scent of sweat and liquor is stuck to your table, and maybe your arms too after you set them down.

The man behind you screams for Sarah in your ear. Then you hear him say, "That will be you next."

Sarah is no pop star, but she has the liquid confidence of one. She bats her black-shadowed eyes and nearly removes her sheer blouse. She might have, if she wasn't holding a microphone, but she starts getting tangled in the cord and it makes removing articles of clothing difficult. Her medium-dark-blonde hair reminds you of Roman's dirty blonde. You imagine Roman at a karaoke night again, standing on stage in a downpour of spotlight. A tank top. Her belly button ring glittering. Her hair down. Not brushed. Her mouth a perfect O.

Sarah sings her last line and smacks her ass so hard you feel the sting, and the audience whistles, slams beer bottles against the bar, and stomps their booted feet. Even some middle-aged women whistle and clap their hands, mirror images of the men beside them. The spotlight catches a few flashes from some of her rings. She has finished singing, but Julia still has to shout over the crowd so you can hear her. She cups her manicured fingers around her mouth and says you're up next. Sarah bows and almost tumbles off the stage. You remember that you are in your own body.

When Roman said she'd take you to karaoke, you were sixteen. She asked what you'd sing. You told her, 'Smells Like Teen Spirit,' even though that was a lie. You changed your mind a few months later. You would sing 'I Want It That Way' instead.

You think of all the things that Roman has been: unhealed little-girl fingers, cocaine bits left on counters, a memory she'd never love. You think of all the things she left behind: some kind of sloppy harem, bad habits that eat you apart, rules for when she's gone.

The man with the beard and microphone says Sarah's a gem and the crowd goes wild. He calls your name. You're up.

Julia says, "Take a drink. It'll help," so you listen to her and take a big sip of the beer she ordered you and almost choke. She adds, "You're a rock star. Go kill 'em!"

You nod your head because it's hard to swallow, and you spit whatever you didn't swallow on the already-stained floor before you walk up to the stage.

The man behind you shouts, "That's not very ladylike."

You crack your knuckles before taking the microphone from the man up front and make sure not to trip over the cord as you walk the one step to the stage.

The light above you crowds your eyes, so it's hard to see the small TV that the lyrics roll across. It's set up on a second wobbly table on the far corner of the tiny stage. Faces in the crowd look like little ping pong balls, and you try to keep them that way because if you think of them as anything more personal, you might throw up on one of them, and that would be even less ladylike.

The space on the floor ahead of you is crowded. People. Tables. Beer. A waitress with lined lips and a rat's nest in her hair tripping between them. You think about how, one day, after everything she had done for you, Roman was a story facedown. And then you couldn't tell if you missed her enough, if you missed her at all, or if sometimes you missed her more than you should on account of the first two. And now you find that, years later, she's still sometimes a catch-your-breath moment. Sometimes a good riddance. Sometimes she's grief-shaped, and you know what that looks like, but you don't entirely know what it is.

Julia doesn't know that you drank peach Fanta mixed with too much vodka before coming out tonight. When she called, you said sure, you were ready to go, and knew that when she showed up in twenty minutes, you'd have to pretend like you wanted to do this.

You know Julia from another bar where she tends and you drink. One night you told her she doesn't look as old as she is. She said that was very sweet of you, but she's also not that old. She said you two should go out, and asked you to karaoke after you'd ordered three or four drinks, but that still wasn't drunk enough for you so you told her no, you don't sing. Then Julia got a raise because it was her four-year anniversary there. She asked about the scar on your arm. The trivia machine made some dinging noises to the left of you. Another bartender dropped a glass behind the counter. You told her most girls get scars. She brought up karaoke again when she handed you another mixed drink. You finally told her yes, you'd go, because she deserved to celebrate.

You know that's why she's excited tonight, because she hopes to see you do what you never do. She thinks that's special.

You must have missed the announcement. You didn't hear the man introduce you, but you notice the lyrics to 'I Want It That Way' start rolling across the screen. The plain karaoke background music has started playing, and that old man with the grimy dollar bill in the audience starts to cheer you on, waving it around, above his head, like it's going to be the thing that makes you a star. A few other men in the crowd clap, but mostly everyone's watching, waiting, except Julia who hasn't stopped shouting woohoo at you. She is smudging her lip gloss a little with her hands cupped around her mouth. You appreciate her enthusiasm, because you are supposed to, even if it is sadder than silence.

Still missing. You miss your chance to sing the first yeah. Your mouth is dry and you have to sing in front of, like, thirty people, or maybe more, but you can't, it's not working, which means you aren't sure if it works at all. The little TV words light up, and you command yourself to say each one out loud, and you don't know what it sounds like when you do, but you think of your lips like an O, not perfect, and how you wouldn't drink any more beer even if you could right now because you know you'd definitely throw up, and you shouldn't let Julia down.

You remove your fingers, close your eyes, and words like syrup finally come out, if only by memory. Half the song is questions, and they are easy to remember, so you say them maybe too loud. You hear the bright, burning split of the speaker's feedback, making people jump. You pull back your voice and come close to simply speaking the end of the song, but in a variety of wrong keys you can't control. A cough caught in your throat. Dewy sweat on your skin. You wonder how Roman would finish her song.

On the last line, you open your eyes and take a heavy breath. You notice for the first time the woman in the audience next to the dollar man. She's round like a ripe peach and her hair is dyed a fake, brown-blonde, so bad that it's fried and fuzzy and curly around her face. She's dressed in a camo jacket, you can't see her pants under the table, and she's got three empty glasses in front of her while she hugs the man's arm that isn't holding the cash he threatens you with. You hope more than anything that she's not who you turn out to be.

You set the mic down on the mud-stained floor. You don't try and take off your shirt like Sarah, but you do take the hair tie off your wrist and wrap it tightly around a sloppy knot you've just formed on the top of your head. No one in the crowd cheers for you. You walk through rows of tables, push against arms, trip on feet, you don't care. You don't look to see if the man will give you the dollar. Julia is standing, blocking him, her arms hangered wide like she wants a celebratory hug.

You push into her space, so dishonest, and you press against her chest, so tightly, she doesn't even realize she is a sing-along song tonight. You take her hair down from her ponytail and run your fingers through it. Something unapologetic about her face makes her almost look like Roman in these shadows. You kiss her fiercely, your lips caught in the sticky burn of her lip gloss. Her wet, shiny mouth half-parted like an open wound when she kisses back with her tongue. Her hungry breath. Your bare face. You push until you can hardly breathe, then you close your mouth. You keep it shut. You let go.

SLUT

WE'RE SMOKING WEED IN MY dad's truck, parked in the garage. Talking about how Lanie was a slut, stoned on coke. Before I was a slut, stoned on coke.

"Lanie's a slut," Bea emphasizes.

I put on some Cyndi Lauper and hand the joint to Bea. She presses it against her lips and her hot pink mouth stains a ring around the end.

I agree and say yeah, she is.

At only thirteen, Lanie has already snuck out of her house to sleep with three different boys. Boys with dirty mustaches and worn skin. Boys who ride broken city buses and don't have their own beds to sleep in.

"Donaven said Lanie called one of the boys on his house phone one night." Bea says they talked for ten minutes. Lanie asked his middle name. When her parents went to bed, she left the house because he told her he'd be parked at a gas station just a block from where she lived. She had to stop to tie her shoelace that had come undone in the dark because the streetlights were burnt out. "Then he fucked her in his car in the dark empty parking lot out there on that main road."

"Yeah," I add, "and he never even told her his middle name."

We laugh with airy breath. I take back the joint and touch it to my own lips, rubbing my tongue all against the pink. I don't tell Bea, but I also know that the boy was eighteen.

Bea reaches her hands out, all grabby, because she's begging. I take one more hit before she makes me hand it back. Bea blows a thin cloud. She nearly whispers, "I heard she's stoned on coke most days now."

I say yeah, I've heard that too.

Bea thinks it's true though. Bea won't admit it, but she doesn't know what a cokehead looks like, so she's relying on what boys her age have said. That, and what she believes to be intuition.

Bea says she doesn't like Cyndi Lauper. "She grew up Catholic."

I take out the CD and let the truck stay silent. Bea doesn't say if she likes the silence better or not. I let it sit.

I don't tell Bea about how I know that Lanie's older brother deals cocaine. Lanie told me herself that he made it easy to get a hold of, and that's why she does it. And it's none of Bea's business, but I've sat next to Lanie when she did it. A group of us crowded around the square, Japanese-style coffee table on the living room floor of hers with a few boys, pouring coke into lines and dividing it up with some hot pink gift cards to Claire's, leftover from Christmas, and even when our lines weren't straight, those boys rolled dollar bills up against their noses and snorted it all. And what's also none of Bea's business, so I won't tell her, is that Lanie and the boys offered me some too, which was very sweet since they didn't have to, and once I got the coke in my nose just right, my mouth, my gums, my throat all numb, I was suddenly next to three people I loved so much. One of the boys started touching Lanie, and I laughed because we all laughed, and then he went up her skirt and it seemed like such a nice thing to do. A small part of me thought maybe I was supposed to tell him to stop, but I didn't since I sort of wanted someone that close to me too.

Bea passes what's left of the joint, really just a small nub now, that I don't think can even be smoked anymore. The pink ring smoldered out a while ago. I push it against my bare thigh until it burns out completely. A small crater forms in my skin, shiny bits of blood surfacing in the wound, but I don't let it phase me.

"Edgy," she says when she looks at the damage I've done.

I start flipping through the pile of CDs in my dad's center console, deciding which to put on next. Bea looks down at my hands and the plastic cases, at what choice I might make. With the way her eyes scrunch up, she might be wondering if I will consult her, but I've already decided I won't. I pass another album from Cyndi Lauper and think about how the singer ran away from home as a teenager, after she was expelled from school. With her dog named Sparkle, she went to the woods to try and find herself. I wonder if she ever did find out who she was. From the side, I see Bea's lip curl up in disgust.

The last thing I think of that I don't tell Bea is that if Lanie fucked a boy in a car, it's not actually because she's a slut. It's because she's powerful. She's learned how to take desire and danger and turn them into envy, and if she's envied, then she's in control, which is something I know we all want, but I'm sure Bea could never admit.

THE BASEMENT

Dust and wood panels. Musty carpet. Finished basement.
Wildlife portraits hang in brown frames.
A fabric couch. Blanket on the floor.
Box TV lights splash on shadowed walls.
Daddy and I are watching one of those investigative journalism shows
on the public television.

NARRATOR: [voice-over] Clara just moved out of the home of her mother, Alice, who spent all of Clara's life presenting herself as different people to her friends and family. Clara wants to confront her now.

CLARA BARLOWE: I remember feeling isolated, like I was some sort of dark mark on her life, but it's time to face it. I want to talk to my mother about my childhood, or about her adulthood, I guess.

ALICE DAUGHERTY: I've always loved my daughter. You know, when you've made something that is such a perfect version of yourself, you have to love it.

I'm spread across the couch,
Daddy's in the red pleather chair to my right.
Hands on lap, mouth zipped shut.
The television interview runs.

221

He likes to record this show—two used VHS tapes
are on the ground.
A stack of board games under his
side table—we used to play Monopoly.

*ALICE DAUGHERTY: I suppose I was living a few lives. I was one
person at work, another with Clara's father Mark, someone else with my
relatives, and then a fourth with my friends. Some of these people knew
and some didn't.*

"Any guy you're trying ta get intimate with's
gonna have to come through me," he once said.
What he meant is that he has a gun. He likes to show it off.

CLARA BARLOWE: Did you ever ask yourself what you were doing?
ALICE DAUGHERTY: I didn't have an option to.
CLARA BARLOWE: Why not?
ALICE DAUGHERTY: It was the sixties.

Sometimes he rests it on his shoulder and cocks it, a big shotgun.
Shiny barrel. Slick lever.
I can tell he likes the way it feels.

*NARRATOR: Alice had dated white men before she met the father of
her daughter, but she says those men disappointed her. They always fell
through on their promises.*
*ALICE DAUGHERTY: Vaughn, my ex who was white like me, told
me about his travels. He'd tell me about high society. He wore expensive
brands and drove a nice car, but when it came time to include me in the
life he promised me, he couldn't because he spent all the money he had
acting like a millionaire, embarrassed that he wasn't. I felt like I was on
the outside looking in, even if what I was looking at was all fake. In a*

way, those years that I spent with Vaughn were years I was in a foreign country.

I like the way Joseph feels.
His skin's real smooth. His lips wet like mine.
I like to rest him on my shoulder.
But he's Black.

ALICE DAUGHERTY: I guess I was used to foreign countries when I met Mark, so at first, I was happy to be in territory I didn't know. But soon, unknown terrain becomes a challenge. My mother would never accept Mark's color—this was in the sixties, when discrimination was especially high.

Daddy doesn't know that I sneak out on Friday nights.
He's too busy playin' poker upstairs with the guys who have
Confederate flag tattoos like him. We haven't played
Monopoly in a long time. He tells me
no, I can't date. He tells me
I'm too young.
But our basement has a door to the backyard.

NARRATOR: [voice-over] So Clara's birth presented some challenges to Alice's different lives.

I met Joseph at the department store I work at.
He was buying his momma a new pair of shoes.
It was her birthday.
He told me to meet him in the parking lot.

ALICE DAUGHERTY: My coworkers didn't know about Clara because I never spent time with them outside of work. With Mark, we only hung

out with his friends who were Black people. I didn't live with my family, but when I did see them, my mother never told them about my daughter. It's like my life just went on as it had before when there was no Clara and no Mark. My mother never met Mark. My friends didn't even know about my baby, really. I was childless to most people.
CLARA BARLOWE: My aunt Mary found out about me though. She made it clear that she did not like the way my mother hid me.
NARRATOR: [voice-over] Clara's aunt Mary has her own thoughts on her sister's behavior, and the way it impacted her niece, and she wants to talk to Clara about them today.

> I'm pregnant. I know I must be. Haven't bled
> in a few months... It's kind of nice.

MARY TAYLOR: You have—
CLARA BARLOWE: What?

> I know this is not good though, being pregnant.

MARY TAYLOR: --in my opinion--

> Daddy'd kill me.

CLARA BARLOWE: Yeah?

> He loves hunting wolves.

MARY TAYLOR: --an attitude toward white people.

> We don't have any paintings of wolves up on the basement walls.

CLARA BARLOWE: Oh?

Just some deer in a field and birds flyin' over water.

MARY TAYLOR: Yeah. You're very bitter towards them.

Docile creatures.

CLARA BARLOWE: Maybe.

Wolves will dominate other dog-kinds in areas where they are both at.

MARY TAYLOR: Where do you think it comes from?

Daddy's like that.

CLARA BARLOWE: I think it comes from understanding white people and the way they think.

And I think Joseph's way more like Daddy than he thinks.

MARY TAYLOR: Okay.

Daddy's got an ashtray receptacle of some sorts next to his chair, of course.

CLARA BARLOWE: I guess I know that because I grew up with my mother though.

For any cigarettes he burns.

MARY TAYLOR: And?

He doesn't go outside for any of that.

CLARA BARLOWE: And, I mean, the way she—

Stays right in the basement.

MARY TAYLOR: *No, I'm wondering how white people think. What would you say about that?*

When we lay there watching the television together,
I notice the burning.
Sometimes he turns the lights off and then
it's just the TV and cigarettes
lighting up the basement.
Then it's hard not to notice them.

CLARA BARLOWE: *Well, it's more like how they don't think.*

Joseph doesn't care that I don't smoke. Haven't drank.
Doesn't care that he was my first.
He tucks my hair behind my ear before he kisses me.

MARY TAYLOR: *Oh.*

Makes me blush.

CLARA BARLOWE: *Because all they see are colors and they won't get past them. The colors stop them from thinking.*

Joseph's momma doesn't like me either.
Says I'm like a battle not worth fighting.

MARY TAYLOR: *Is that what it's like?*

Daddy thinks he's protecting me
with his rules.
That's what he claims it is anyway.

ALICE DAUGHERTY: When I first looked at you, I couldn't believe I made you. You came from my womb. I look at you and think about how you wouldn't be here if it wasn't for me.

CLARA BARLOWE: [voice-over] Friends have asked me how my mother kept so many lives straight, and how I navigated them all. I didn't want to, but I guess I got skilled at adapting.

Joseph wears charming like a necklace.

He'll say suave things that just pick me up off my feet.

He wraps hands twice the size of mine against my shoulders

and pulls me in against his chest,

makes my breath go swoosh.

I'm glad he's the father of my baby.

ALICE DAUGHERTY: I've never told you all this before.

CLARA BARLOWE: Yeah, I know.

ALICE DAUGHERTY: It shouldn't have been, but it was dangerous. Our life. I was trying to protect you.

Daddy's sitting next to me on the couch.

I think about telling him all this—he's gonna find out eventually.

Then I look at the Monopoly box on the floor, under the side table.

Show's almost over. I ask him if he wants to play Monopoly.

Like old times.

ALICE DAUGHERTY: People wanted to ostracize him—destroy us.

CLARA BARLOWE: You mean white people.

ALICE DAUGHERTY: Yeah.

Daddy ignores me. Turns off the television.

He grunts. Says, "She shouldn'ta been with him in the first place."

This story, "The Basement," was inspired by Gregory Crewdson's art of the same name, "The Basement" (2014), and the FRONTLINE episode #1505, "Secret Daughter."

GHOST STORIES

YOU HAVEN'T BEEN IN THIS basement for years, and it's easy to remember why. Everything sounds like rats and smells like mold. No one knows where things are. Your mother has not cleaned the space in a few decades, so it's hard to know what's even here. It's a graveyard of memories that everyone's nervous to resurrect.

Your mother told you she planned to throw everything out soon and asked if you wanted any of it. You didn't, but your boyfriend said looking at it could be fun.

"I'll go with you," he said.

So you told your mother you'd stop by next Saturday, and then your boyfriend had to work, so now you are stuck here by yourself.

You step over a rolled-up race track carpet, some small dolls with yanked-out hair, and a loose Pound Puppy with stains. You remember all this stuff, and some part of you misses it, although you're not sure why.

You manage to get to the plastic, see-through, storage boxes stacked in the back. The one on top has butterfly-shaped candles you never lit, small stuffed animals with handmade crowns, and your Marilyn Monroe Fur Fantasy doll. The box below it has a pink and purple plastic beaded doorway divider and a few rolled up band posters. You don't remember which bands they might be. There's a folded black and gold t-shirt that says Blow Kisses Not Coke. You didn't take that dumb t-shirt off for the two days you were locked in your room doing coke. The irony was not lost on you. At some point during those days, you laughed for twenty minutes straight.

You're sick to your stomach.

The box at the bottom of the stack has a Bop-It with a broken part, a very old Super Nintendo that hasn't had a good blow in well over two decades, and a few hot pink, lime green, and royal purple beady buddy geckos you made at the end of second grade, next to a bag of leftover pony beads.

Then you see your old Tamagotchi. The relic is navy blue with three yellow buttons, and you had been sure it was lost forever. You move boxes to grab it, but when you get to it you find that it won't turn on.

You remember how, in third grade, Kelsey had a Tamagotchi she brought to school every day just to tease you by making sure you saw it. She'd pull it out and make it do a trick that she wouldn't show. Hers was your favorite color, pink, and she put a bow on the keychain it hung from. By the fall, nearly everyone in the fourth grade had their own Tamagotchi. Except you. You wanted one, desperate to have something of your own to carry and show off, but your begging fell on deaf ears—until Christmas Eve, when your grandma handed you a small box of what had to be socks, you were sure, but then you opened your very own Tamagotchi instead. You put your grandma in a devastating bear hug and kissed her cheek an indefinite number of times until she pushed you away.

You didn't realize it before, but now that it's in front of you, you know you missed this toy. It may be fun to play again. You put it in your pocket, leave the boxes where they are, and tell your mother you're not interested in anything—she can throw it all out.

Back at your place, you find a pen that can push the tiny reset button on the back of the oval-shaped technology. When you do this, a thin line splits the screen, and then your small, digital egg appears. You say, Aww, and tap at the screen as if you are petting it. You say hi to it as if you're greeting an old friend.

Your boyfriend walks in the door without knocking and asks what you're up to. You show him the Tamagotchi and say, "Look what I found at my mother's." He walks closer to inspect. You hold out the device, which has a pastel, beaded chain hanging from it, crafted by nine-year-old you. The digital egg begins wiggling until it hatches and you almost make a small squeal out of disbelief. Your boyfriend notices your excitement and tells you to chill. He says, "Seriously, it's fake."

You tell your boyfriend it just hatched and now it's a baby. You'll have to feed it and play games with it, but find that what you're looking forward to most is actually the new sense of purpose you feel. You like that something will rely on you.

"Did you name it?"

"Not yet."

He tells you he's gonna go watch the football game on your TV because he doesn't have cable like you do.

You try to play another game with the creature, but it doesn't want to, so you press the scold button. You plan to train it while it's young. Then the screen zips shut, like an old box television set that's shutting down. You gasp, your boyfriend calls out what, and you can't make out any real words but just mumbled sounds of despair. You push a few buttons, and it turns back on, so you give another sigh, but one of relief this time. Your boyfriend doesn't ask any more questions, and you can hear the television in the other room get louder. You say hi to your little guy again and press a few more buttons.

This goes on for a few days. Your boyfriend asks when he'll get to spend time with you as you're curled up on the couch in front of some reality TV show, and you tell him that you guys *are* spending time together. He says that you're too busy playing with your egg.

You say, "It's not an egg anymore. It's almost a teen."

He asks what that even means and you don't answer.

When you had brought your Tamagotchi to school after the New Year, you found that no one cared. Nearly everyone had one by then. Still, you took the creature to lunch with you, making sure to feed it. You took it to the playground and made it do tricks. You hid it in your desk, pressing buttons during lessons and assignments to keep your friend alive. Your mother worked weeknights then, so you'd sit in bed and watch reruns of late-night talk shows and PBS cartoons. You listened to your albums on repeat. You colored in the blonde ladies' hair with pink and orange markers in the magazine cutouts taped to your wall until all the women had been transformed. You wrote No Boys Allowed on your jeans with a permanent marker. You pressed Tamagotchi buttons and watched your little friend grow up.

In the winter, you made honor roll and your mother took you to McDonald's to celebrate. You sat in the play area, watching the snow fall outside through the big glass walls around you. You remember it feeling like a shaken snow globe. You held your Tamagotchi up so he could see the flurries too. You ran off to slide down the big, yellow slide.

When you got home and couldn't find your toy anywhere, you told your mother you had to go back. You must have left your Tamagotchi at the restaurant.

"Oh, I'm so sorry, honey."

You told her you had to go back.

Even in the dark of the night, you saw her shrug.

She said, "It's okay. That's a little kid's toy and you're a big girl now."

On the fourth night, you wake up, unsure of what's happening at first. When you realize the commotion is coming from your side table, your heart skips a beat, and you immediately reach out for your baby, who you've since named Joel. He is beeping and flashing. You turn your small lamp on so you can investigate better, but you quickly realize you have no idea how to fix it. You don't want to restart it, fearing the restart will eliminate Joel, so you just smash the buttons on the front, hoping if you do it enough that something about your aimless aggression will fix it.

Your Tamagotchi continues to beep and buzz and blink for the next hour, and you've started crying and choking on your own spit. You want to call your boyfriend, to ask for advice, but it's three in the morning and he wouldn't know what to do anyway. After another twenty minutes, the screen stops flashing, the line zips open, and Joel reappears. Thank goodness. You feed him a burger, hoping that will make up for the trauma, and tell him to go to sleep. It's late. You set him down, and roll back over in bed.

You don't remember this glitch happening when you were younger, so you chalk it up to age. This thing's nearly twenty years old. You're lucky they made stuff more durable back then. There would be no chance that something made now could ever be resurrected in twenty years.

When you wake up, you immediately check on Joel, and he's sound asleep. You're glad he got some rest. You, on the other hand, feel nauseous from last night's ordeal. You go into the bathroom and throw up, despite not having thrown up in years.

You call your boyfriend to tell him about what happened.

"It was weird."

"Yeah," he says.

"I mean, don't you think so?"

"Yeah. I already said that."

"Okay, I guess." You add, "I hope it doesn't happen again."

"Sure."

He doesn't get it. You walk back to your room to grab Joel who you find awake, having grown older while you were away.

You're upset you missed this milestone and your boyfriend, whose voice is tucked between your shoulder and ear, groans. You tell him you love him and you gotta go, so you hang up.

The next day, your Tamagotchi makes a weird screeching noise while you're at work. The coworkers who already think you're strange start whispering. There are cliques, like in high school, and no one has accepted you into theirs. Last month, the women made plans to go to the bar without you, in front of you. But this noise from Joel is different from the noise the other night, so you have to excuse yourself to take him outside. You become really concerned because you've done a great job training him, and he's grown up a bit, and the last thing you want is for him to disappear.

You don't try to call your boyfriend. You know he doesn't get it—he never gets it.

You spend twenty more minutes outside, shushing the egg and trying not to throw up from anxiety.

When your boyfriend comes over for dinner, he brings a large pizza and kisses you on your lips. He backs off.

"You taste a little like vomit?" He says it like a question.

You did throw up earlier, before you fixed the Tamagotchi. You realize that you never brushed your teeth.

"I'm sorry," you say. "Excuse me." You walk to the bathroom to do it.

"Is everything okay?" He calls from down the hall.

You nod your head but he can't see.

He appears in your bathroom doorway as you brush. He puckers his lips and squints at you. He waits a beat, then quietly asks, "Could you be pregnant?"

You stop brushing, your mouth full of toothpaste and saliva, and you spit it hard into the sink. "No. I just haven't been feeling well lately." You turn your back to him. He knows you're out of birth control, but you're sure that's not it. Your boyfriend's been pulling out, so the sickness must be anxiety over Joel. The anxiety of loving someone so much it hurts. You've never felt that before, but you're sure this is it now.

Prior to now, you had never had an actual boyfriend. You looked for one at high school dances, feral house parties, and mile-road walks. You gave them what you thought they wanted when you developed nudes and bought dresses like ones the movie stars wore. You tried not to hurt them. Guys that is. Then you stopped giving them anything at all. At some point, you had nothing left to give.

When a friend had an extra ticket and invited you to a football game, you went because it was free, not because you like football. When your friend conveniently left out that others were joining you, you met your boyfriend. They say that's how to find a partner—stop looking, and someone shows up. He drank a few beers and explained the game. You don't remember how the game gets won. He asked for your number because he said he liked the way you listened, and you gave it to him. Like a cat you feed once, he never went away. At twenty-eight, you've been with him for two years now.

For what it's worth, you had never had a girlfriend, either. You don't think a woman would be easier.

Your boyfriend's not convinced, so you agree to make sure you aren't pregnant. Joel is enough responsibility anyway, especially now that he glitches repeatedly. It's a lot of work to worry and troubleshoot.

You buy a pregnancy test from CVS. You pee on the stick. While you are waiting, you make sure to check what means yes. The pamphlet says two lines mean yes. After the time is up, there is only one line.

"I'm not pregnant," you tell your boyfriend when he calls.

"You sure?"

"Yes. I took a test."

"That's great news."

You say, "I told you—I'm not feeling well."

He lets an awkward silence grow between you, which is most likely time he spends thinking about you and Joel. You don't say anything about it.

"Well, feel better," he finally says.

Sure. You tell him you have to go, you love him, talk to him later, and all that jazz. You hang up the phone and crawl into bed, under your comforter, and let the light from your little egg illuminate the cocoon you create for yourself.

Joel has gotten sick. You know this because of the skull icon that has appeared. You've been adamant about picking up his poop, so you know his illness must be from overfeeding. You've given him many snacks because you like making him happy. You whisper to him, "I promise I'll cut back on the snacks, baby. I don't want you sick. Please get better." He just became an adult yesterday.

Joel's face becomes a pixelated form, unmoving, and you feel a gag rise in your throat. "I'll be right back," you tell him, and you emerge from your shell with barely enough time to get to your hallway bathroom and throw up in the sink. You're both sick. Who's going to take care of you two?

Your boyfriend doesn't believe that you took a pregnancy test. He wants you to take one again so he can see. You're pissed he thinks this is okay, but you know you're not pregnant, and if this will be the only way to get him off your back, you tell him to buy one himself and bring it over later. You think you might break up with him after this whole ordeal anyway.

Joel glitched again last night. No noises, just bright flashing that kept you up. You don't want to hide him in your nightstand, so you've started setting him on your pillow with you. You stayed up until he finally came back on. You still aren't sure why it's happening, and are also still worried it will completely fail one day and Joel will permanently disappear.

Your boyfriend stops by with the test. You tell him you'll piss on the stick, but can he give you some privacy, and his face makes it seem like he doesn't trust that it'll be your piss or something. Who else's would you have in there? Why would you lie about this?

You lock your bathroom door, and start the process again. You've got the stick in its little contraption doing its magic, and you're just waiting for the time to finish so you can show your boyfriend you're not pregnant.

Your boyfriend yells at you, "Wait—how much water have you drank recently?"

"I don't know. Not since lunch."

"Okay, you should be good."

"What's the problem?"

He says he's looking at the directions, and they say too much water could dilute the urine and make a false negative.

You realize you bought a case of water with your last test and drank a whole bottle before taking it. You start to worry—it couldn't be. You pull Joel from your pocket and stroke him.

"I think the time is up," your boyfriend says.

"Maybe a little longer." You pace the small bathroom as the stick sits on the counter. Your boyfriend groans, but doesn't tell you no, because he wants the answer to be certain this time.

You make Joel do some tricks, proud of what he's learned, and after two minutes your boyfriend bangs on the door and tells you the time is definitely up. You roll your eyes.

You give Joel a kiss, gently place him back in your pocket with his head poking out enough to still breathe, grab the stick from the counter, and hand it to your boyfriend when you emerge. He says, "Did you look?"

You tell him no, because you already know the answer.

He looks down at the test and says, "Oh shit."

It doesn't sound like a good *oh shit*. He lifts the stick, holds it in front of your face, and shows you two lines, very clear.

You shake your head. It must be wrong.

Your boyfriend stares at you, your throat closes, you can't breathe. He starts rubbing your back lightly. You are buoyant.

You immediately regret drinking that water, as if the water caused a pregnancy.

You say it can't be true.

Your boyfriend says, "Look, it'll be okay," like he's an actor in a movie, playing a part. He awkwardly laces his fingers through yours, but you pull away. You can tell he's panicking because he only touches you softly when he panics. He leans in to kiss you, which makes you want to puke again, even though you don't actually need to this time. He says, "I won't leave you."

You almost want him to. Any decision you make might be easier that way, otherwise you've got too many to worry about now. He holds the stick up again, and it feels like a wave rises inside you, crashes against you, and floods tears to your eyes where a small pool collects at their corners. He guides your body down, so you two are sitting on the floor outside your bathroom, leaning against each other's shoulders. He whispers, "I love you." He puts his hand on top of yours. "We can get married and have the baby. You're not alone." You don't think that makes you feel better. He smells your hair when he finishes his sentence. Snot drips down your lip and sticks to your chin.

Your pocket starts beeping and your boyfriend groans. "Right fucking now?" he asks, like you chose for Joel to glitch at this moment.

"Look, I didn't ask for it to do this."

You pull out Joel and realize it's not a glitch. It's a devastating noise that you didn't remember, and now that you realize what's happening you shout out a resounding no. Your crying gets uglier—Joel has died. The screen shows a small angel blinking softly and you throw the egg against the opposite wall. You jerk away from your boyfriend and with your whole chest you moan, curling forward into your knees. All those snacks you fed him were too much to recover from.

You kept him alive the entire time he glitched, made sure he survived and treated him well, but he still died in the end. What was even the point?

Your boyfriend reluctantly starts rubbing your back and you smack his hand away.

You tell him, "Don't."

You'd been astonished to find the Tamagotchi in that storage box because you had thought it was gone forever, thrown away in a McDonald's garbage bin. But no, your mother had hidden it from you.

It wasn't until you started playing it again that you remembered how, back before the loss, you'd sometimes stop taking care of it. You would starve it, you'd let it shit all over and not clean it up, and then you'd scold it for being unhappy. When it died its sad, angel death, you would hatch a new egg and do it all over again, sometimes over and over. Those times, the kill was intentional.

Two weeks have passed, and your boyfriend is sitting next to you on the couch, asking if you want to start brainstorming names.

"It's a little early for that, isn't it?"

He shrugs. "What's it going to hurt? We'll need to pick one eventually."

He wants to think of boys' and girls' names, but you think that's a waste because you know it's a girl. The energy inside you is volatile, which means that's the only thing it can be.

You've got some old-timey movie on TV because there's no game tonight, which is the only reason your boyfriend is even talking to you right now. He starts to list names, ones that you know are unrealistic. He says, "Adam, Lucas, John." He turns the volume down to make sure you hear him better. "Rochelle, Ava, Gwendolyn." He lists traditionally masculine names and stereotypically pretty names. Names you would expect a man to suggest for his child.

"Norma," you say.

For a moment he is silent. This tells you that he's either uninterested, or he thinks you're kidding, but you aren't. This is the only name you are sure of. He puts his hand in the front pocket of his pants, like he's searching for something.

The movie switches to commercials and one for some handheld video game comes on with the screen lit up in flashy colors. The game is new, so younger children would know what it is, but you don't, and you don't bother listening to find out. Your Tamagotchi has been sitting on your coffee table since you threw it, cracked. You won't touch it.

Your boyfriend finally takes his hand out of his pants, and he's got a small, fake-velvet box that he hands to you. He says, "I wanted to give you this, you know, since we'll be getting married now." You don't have to open it to know it's a tiny, generic diamond ring from the mall jewelry store.

"Thanks."

When you leave it on your lap, untouched, he says, "Aren't you going to put it on?"

So you open the box. Stare at the gem. You were right— it's tiny and generic. You wonder who you are in his eyes.

He slides the ring on your finger and it's so loose it wants to fall off no matter what you do. With his arms wrapped around you, he presses one of his hands against yours and holds the ring in place. But you know he can't hold it there forever. What will he do then?

The next commercial is for a plastic makeup kit so little girls can play pretend. It shows a pink, fabric bag covered in embroidered hearts, full of little toy mascara, blush, and lipsticks. A girl with a fake tiara smiles at herself while she looks in the mirror and pretends to apply them. This is a toy you recognize because all of your girlfriends had it growing up. You know how phony it is, but the things that train girls while they're young always are.

You think of your daughter, Norma, and how one day she'll be sixteen, dating an eighteen-year-old. It won't matter that they met a year before, when he wasn't an adult. It won't matter that she sprayed herself in candy perfume before the party she went to without your permission. It won't matter that she wore the short skirt, the rhinestone belly button ring, and the glossy lipstick on the night they met. He will kiss her, she will think he loves her, and you'll still call the cops on him. Because if you don't, she'll one day end up like every other woman, a vanishing afterthought, and you'd rather do what it takes to make her angry, feral, and problematic instead.

You know that there is no winning, so there's no reason to play by the rules of the game.

CONTENT WARNINGS

Your Mother, 1981: Will Work for Shoes
Prostitution

Lena, 2000: Cross to Bear
Alcohol

You, 2003: Centerfold Wannabe
Child pornography

Katie, 2010: Bloody Mary
Stripping, death

Roman, 2000: Don't Bother
Sexual assault

Kia, 2002: Period Sex
Blood

You, 2004: Crushing
Pedophilia

Daria with her friend Monica, 2008: It Doesn't Take Much
Sexual assault, idea of stripping, anxiety

Roman, 2003: We're All Strangers
Prison, rape, drugs, prostitution

Kia, 2004: These Are Not Love Letters
Death

You, 2007: Ladylike
Assault, idea of car crashes

Crystal, 2005: First Date
Alcohol

Crystal, 2007: Anatomy of Desire
Idea of death

Crystal, 2008: Locate the Heart Line
Infidelity

Catalogue Carly, 2005: Young and Reckless
Pregnancy, abortion, infidelity, alcohol, suicide

Kia, 2003: Loser
Alcohol, anxiety

Lena, 2004: Tarnished
Infidelity

You, 2009: Perfect Fit
Anxiety, body image

Kia, 2003: Hunger
Eating disorder

Jessica, 2006: Boys Make the Same Mistakes
Infidelity

Your Mother, 2003: Berries, Blood, Wheat
Pedophilia

NOTES

Songs and their musical artists referenced include:

"Take a Bow" by Madonna
"More Than a Feeling" by Boston
"Wheel in the Sky" by Journey
"It's Not Over" by Daughtry
"Smells Like Teen Spirit" by Nirvana
"I Want It That Way" by Backstreet Boys

The photo referenced on page 119 was a photo of Evelyn McHale's death published in LIFE magazine in May, 1947.

The story "The Basement" was inspired by Gregory Crewdson's art of the same name, "The Basement" (2014), and the *FRONTLINE* episode #1505, "Secret Daughter."

VISIT

www.TheWomenExpansion.weebly.com

FOR MORE FUN

ACKNOWLEDGEMENTS

Thank you, thank you, thank you Xavier Iriarte for elevating my writing in beautiful, necessary ways. Thank you Paul Lacoursiere and Emma Kaput for your many reads and continued feedback. For additional close readings that allowed this story to be even better than I thought, I thank Elisabeth "Em" Marcus, Taya Alani, Annie Williams, Melissa Marguerite, and Patrick Peavy. I appreciate you volunteering your time more than you know.

Thank you to my all-women team who make dreams become reality. Lindee Robinson provided the perfect photos and marketing materials. Najla Qamber and Nada Qamber design the homes my words live in (including this interior and cover).

Thanks to Annie Gilson and Peter Markus for continued support. Many of the stories in this collection started as seeds in their classes.

Thank you to my husband Zak.

And more gratitude goes to all the girls I grew up with.